BV16
V. A.

X JD

DOCTOR DARLING

D1198402

LP FIC VER
Vernon, Claire
Doctor Darling /
5359525

32022196288696

DOCTOR DARLING

Claire Vernon

CHIVERS

British Library Cataloguing in Publication Data available

This Large Print edition published by BBC Audiobooks Ltd, Bath, 2010.
Published by arrangement with the Author's Estate..

U.K. Hardcover ISBN 978 1 408 49221 5
U.K. Softcover   ISBN 978 1 408 49222 2

Copyright © Claire Vernon 1962

All rights reserved.

Printed and bound in Great Britain by
CPI Antony Rowe, Chippenham and Eastbourne

CHAPTER ONE

Creena Hall was just putting the cover on her typewriter when the telephone bell shrilled. A tall slim girl with red-gold hair curling round her oval face, she looked younger than her twenty-three years. Maybe because of the eager excited look in her green eyes—perhaps because of her vivacity, for she was always gay and laughing. She was secretary-receptionist at the Pumula Hospital and outside the wide open window, she could see the African sun blazing down out of a cloudless sky.

She answered the telephone and her face was suddenly radiant. 'Dennis . . . darling . . .' she said impulsively—then leaned forward over the low counter and looked down the hospital corridor. No one in sight luckily, for Dennis was always impressing on her the need to be formal during working hours. 'Yes, Dr. Tyson . . .?' she said demurely and was rewarded by his low warm chuckle in her ear.

'That's better, honey . . .' he said softly. 'Just called you to let you know I may be late picking you up tonight for the dance. An emergency op. has just come in . . .'

'But . . . but Dr. McGregor is on call . . .' Creena said instantly.

Dennis grunted. 'He should be but we can't find him anywhere. A straightforward case,

1

luckily. Shouldn't be any complications . . .'

'There never are any—with you . . .' Creena told him proudly.

Again that warm chuckle in her ear. 'Hark at my trumpeter . . .' he teased. 'Anyhow I thought I'd warn you . . . but I know you'll understand. That's the best of having a girl who's a doctor's daughter . . .'

'I always wondered why you ran around with me . . .' Creena teased back.

'Did you?' Dennis's voice was suddenly grave. 'Remind me to tell you one day the real reason.'

He rang off and she sank back in her seat, a familiar sweet breathlessness filling her. Dennis was always such fun—always teasing and joking about the future, but so rarely serious. Yet did she really want him to be serious—yet?

She tidied up the small office, thankful because in Swaziland the working hours were from eight in the morning until half-past four in the afternoon, which always left time for a ride on Snow-White or a walk with the dogs.

The telephone bell shrilled again and she answered it. This time it was her mother's plaintive voice asking her to pick up the groceries from the store.

'I did ask your father, Creena, but you know what he is . . . His head up in the clouds and mundane things like food just don't matter,' she said.

2

elegant head. Quido took her hand gently in his mouth and led her up the narrow steep steps towards the house, looking back at her now and then. Creena went round the back to the stables first—the horses were out in the paddock and Mike was saddling King.

'Hi!' he shouted. 'Coming?'

Creena went to speak to the horses, smiling at her thin, long-legged brother. 'I'm going to have a bath and a beauty treatment . . .'

Grinning, he told her she certainly needed it. 'Going dancing?'

'M'm . . . there's the Charity Ball at Nsingisi . . .'

'Going with Dennis, of course . . .' He spoke over his shoulder but something in his voice made him sound sulky.

'Why don't you like Dennis?' Creena asked abruptly.

Mike's flushed face looked over the horse's back as he walked round him.

'He's all right . . . for girls . . .' he said.

Creena frowned. 'Look, Mike, what do you mean?'

Mike shrugged. 'Just that. He's all right for girls. He likes 'em . . . so they like him.'

'He likes you, Mike . . .'

Mike looked sceptical. 'Oh—yeah?' he drawled. 'Well, you certainly have surprised me. Has he said so?'

Creena blushed. 'No, but . . .' The truth was that Dennis did not like Mike—he considered

7

him spoilt and much too crazy about horses and fishing and shooting. Dennis was always saying that it was a pity Mike didn't work at school with the same fervour as he gave to his hobbies.

Mike swung himself up on King and whistled to the dogs. Creena stood still, watching them walk down the paddock where Mike leant down to unlatch the gate, walk through and then re-latch it. The other two horses looked after him indifferently and then went back to graze. The dogs were barking hysterically—Rudi nearly turning somersaults as he shot through the grass, leaping in the air to look over it to make sure he wasn't being left behind.

Creena walked down the garden towards the house. She shouted to her father who was on his knees by his beloved strawberries and was doubtlessly weeding them. He never left that to the garden boy!

Violet, the housegirl, was in the kitchen, peeling potatoes. She smiled as Creena strolled through it—her white teeth flashing in her brown face. She was wearing a crisply starched white apron round her blue print frock and a small white cap was perched perilously on top of her dark tight curls. Creena hid a smile—she could see that her mother had been on the war-path for Violet was notoriously lax about wearing that little cap. She loathed it.

Creena found her mother sitting on the stoep, knitting and watching the clouds in the blue sky throw dark patches on the mountains. Creena bent and kissed her mother lightly and was rewarded by a warm smile.

'Thanks for picking up the groceries, darling. The water's nice and hot—I told Violet to stoke up the fire . . .' she said. She was a short plumpish woman with greying hair, glasses and a deep dimple in her chin. 'I guessed you'd want to pretty yourself for tonight . . .'

Creena sank into one of the long wicker chairs and relaxed. 'You're so right, Mummy . . .' she said and yawned happily. 'Not that there is any panic—Dennis may be late.'

Her mother sighed, looking at her anxiously. 'Darling, that's the worst of marrying a doctor. I went through all that . . .'

'I know . . .' Creena frowned a little. Why all this sudden emphasis on Dennis today? First Mrs. Isipin—then Mike—and now her mother. There had been no talk of marriage. She stood up. 'I'll go and soak . . . can I borrow some of your bath cubes, Mummy? Mine are finished.'

'Of course, darling. What frock are you wearing?' her mother stopped knitting to look up at her.

'I don't know . . . yet.' Creena confessed. To her, one of the most exciting parts of an evening out was making a slow careful choice of frock. Not that she had so many to choose

9

from—but quite enough to make it an interesting task. She had learned dressmaking in Johannesburg in the evenings while she was at the Secretarial College and those boring lessons had paid off handsomely for now she made nearly all her own clothes. It meant she could have a great many more—for she did not earn very much at the hospital and her parents still had two children to educate so could not help her much financially.

Three hours later, she was sitting in the lounge with her mother. She had chosen a white sheath frock and borrowed some green beads from her mother to twist round her neck. She was waiting for Dennis, trying not to watch the clock, knowing it was not his fault. It was a pity, though, for it would take them at least forty-five minutes to reach the dance . . . but it couldn't be helped. Her mother was knitting a bright red sweater for Norma, who, at that moment, strolled into the room in her dressing-gown, her plump face covered with white cream, her dark brown hair done up in bright rollers. She was fourteen and becoming almost painfully aware of the need to look glamorous. It was something Creena and her parents could not get over—this sudden change in Norma, who—until less than three months before—had only wanted to be riding the horses or playing with the dogs and who, half the time, had to be bullied into changing out of her jeans into a frock.

'Dennis is late . . .' Norma said and added hastily. 'Don't be mad with him, Creena, he can't help it.'

Creena looked at her with some amusement. 'I know he can't . . .'

Norma perched on the arm of the couch. 'He says you are a very understanding person.'

Creena chuckled. 'That's big of him . . .'

Her father stood in the doorway. 'Come and see the moon, Creena. It's a picture.'

'And you be off to bed,' Creena heard her mother say to Norma. Norma had been to a teen-age party the night before and turned up at two o'clock in the morning owing to a puncture in the car she was in. Their mother had been furious yet had recognized it was not Norma's fault but had insisted on an early night for a change.

Creena went out into the dark garden by her father's side. He was a tall thin man with a great shock of white hair and, strangely enough, a red moustache. She tucked her hand through his arm, resting her head against his shoulder, as they gazed silently at the enormous golden globe in the black sky,

'Creena . . .' her father said softly. 'Are you going to marry Dennis?'

Startled, she stared up at the dark shadows on his face that hid his expression. 'He hasn't asked me to . . .'

'But if he does?' her father persisted.

She fidgeted a little. Why didn't everyone

11

leave her alone.

'I don't know, Dad . . . I like him but . . .'

His hand closed over hers suddenly. 'If there is even a shadow of doubt in your mind, darling, then don't marry him,' her father said, his voice quiet still but now urgent. 'You must be very sure . . .'

'You don't like Dennis, Dad, do you?' she said, her voice surprised.

'He's all right . . . but . . .'

She laughed a little. 'Dad—don't let's treat this too seriously. Dennis is one of the few available young men around to go dancing with and and I'm—'

'Conveniently on the spot?' her father asked, his voice dry. 'And very understanding?'

Her cheeks burned. 'I . . . I'm not even sure he loves me . . .'

'You've been going out together for over three years.' Her father sounded quite stern. 'I wish there were more young men available, Creena. It's not right for you to only know Dennis. You've no yard-stick to measure him by. I wish . . . I wish I'd insisted that you got a job in Johannesburg . . . or even went to England to work and meet people.'

'Daddy darling, I'd have hated it,' Creena told him quickly. 'Living in digs and being lonely. I'm much happier here at home.'

He sighed. It sounded quite clearly in the still of the night. 'I still think we haven't been very wise. Dennis is a brilliant young man in many ways but . . .'

They heard the distant sound of a car—the sound grew louder, closer, the bright lights pierced the darkness of the quiet lane and a car turned in over the cattle trap.

'Your young man . . .' Creena's father said. 'I'll get your coat . . .'

Dennis came bounding up the steps towards her. 'Hi—honey . . .' he said, throwing his arms round her and giving her a hug. 'Sorry I'm so late but I was in trouble—big trouble . . .'

The door to the house was wide open, Dennis stood, framed in the bright light and Creena looked at him intently. She wondered if she was seeing him for the first time. Somehow they had drifted into this relationship and now she wondered why such a handsome impressive-looking young man should have chosen her out of all the *talent*, to use Mike's expression, available. He was not so young, either, for he was over thirty, but his face gave an impression of youth. He was tall and very broad-shouldered, his black hair always smooth, his dark eyes sometimes brooding, sometimes alight with laughter. He looked very much alive—you could feel the almost tangible electricity in the air when he entered a room.

Creena's mother brought out the coat for Creena and Dennis was very charming to her. He certainly had a way of making women his slaves, Creena thought with affectionate

13

amusement.

'I'll take great care of her, Mrs. Hall,' he was promising.

'I know you will, Dennis . . .' her mother said happily.

In the car, Creena turned her head. 'What held you up, Dennis?' she asked lazily. 'Complications?'

'Big trouble . . .' he said curtly. 'Mrs. Crampton and McGregor had a fight again.'

Mrs. Crampton! She owned the hospital— or rather her late husband had endowed it and she still helped to finance it and so had a large say in the running of it. A regrettable thing, Creena's father had always said. He and Mrs. Crampton had never seen eye to eye. But Dennis seemed to like the autocratic old lady and got on well with her.

'What over?' Creena asked—watching the bright path slashed through the darkness of the tree-lined road by the headlights.

'I don't know,' Dennis said and somehow, she knew that he lied. 'Anyhow he's gone . . . they had a row and she told him to get out and he said he would and . . . He's driving to Johannesburg tonight . . .'

Creena swivelled round on the seat of the car and stared at him in dismay. 'But he can't just walk out like that . . .'

'Well, he has . . .'

Dennis was slowing up into the main street, driving past the brilliantly lighted hotels,

14

taking the road to Nsingisi.

'Then who's on duty at the hospital—or rather, on call?'

'I got Dr. Pipp to stand in—his wife's mad at me so I'd better dance with her a few times to smooth things over.' Dennis sounded amused.

'Well, if he does go to a dance, he never dances,' Creena said. 'So I don't see why she's mad. She knows a doctor can't help these things. He spends all his time in the bar with his cronies so what is she missing?'

'Status, dear Creena,' Dennis said mockingly. 'She says a woman loses face if she goes to a dance on her own.'

'That's plain silly . . . she knows everyone here and—'

'Well, she is—just plain silly, isn't she?'

Creena snuggled closer to his shoulder. 'I'm glad I'm going with you.'

He laughed. 'Thanks, honey . . .'

They had left the trees behind now and were driving along a wide flat road, brightly lighted by the moonlight. Dennis braked as they reached a sharp corner and the car skidded a little in the dust, he straightened it as they began to drive down the steep drop to a valley below. The short white poles that marked a sheer drop into a rock-clustered ravine showed up clearly and reminded Creena of something. She shivered.

'How is Hugh, Dennis?' she asked. He was a lad of sixteen who had been flung off a car that

15

had taken the corner too fast.

'I hear he's better but he'll never walk again,' Dennis said.

She turned in dismay. 'Hugh—an invalid for life?'

'He's lucky to be alive.'

'Maybe he'd prefer not to be . . .' she said slowly, remembering the strong youngster who had played good rugger and was also mad about cricket. She shivered.

'We all have to do lots of things we'd prefer not to do . . .' Dennis said. Was he being a little pompous, she wondered and was ashamed of herself. 'I'm not enjoying working in a tuppenny halfpenny spot like this . . .'

She was surprised. She had thought he was happy. 'But why—'

'Oh, to you this is paradise, Creena. You've never known anything else. I want to work in a city—I want to specialize but it costs money . . . and that is something I lack . . .' He laughed. 'Maybe I'd better marry a rich girl. Your father got plenty tucked away, darling?'

She looked at him gravely. 'I'm afraid he hasn't.'

Dennis hooted with laughter. 'Where's your sense of humour, honey? I was only kidding you. I don't need to marry money—I'll make it.'

Suddenly she realized something. 'This isn't the way, Dennis . . .'

He looked down at her and did not slow up.

16

'I know—we have to go to Mrs. Crampton's on the way to pick up her grand-daughter, Alisa ...'

'Ailsa?'

'Creena ... I told you ...' Dennis began and hesitated. 'Or didn't I? I am sorry if I didn't, honey, but I promised Mrs. Crampton we'd take Ailsa along tonight. I knew you wouldn't mind ...'

Mind? Creena thought miserably of what Norma, her sister had said. Dennis had said she was very understanding. But how understanding must you be?

'Ailsa is only a child ... she doesn't want to go to the Charity Ball.'

'Doesn't she?' Dennis was amused. 'You'd be surprised. She's crazy to go.'

'But Dennis, she's only fifteen ...'

'Sixteen and three days, darling,' Dennis corrected her. 'And very grown-up for her age ...' he drawled. 'Mrs. Crampton says the poor child is so bored here and there is nothing to do and no young man she can trust so—'

'So we have to take her along ...' Creena said bitterly.

It was absurd the disappointment that flooded her. Ailsa was a precocious brat ... no other words to describe her.

'Why, honey.' Dennis sounded dismayed. 'I believe you mind ...' He braked, nearly flinging Creena through the wind-screen, and then stopped the car by the side of the road, turning to take her in his arms.

His kisses were warm and ardent. He kissed her throat, her bare shoulders, her mouth. 'Honey—I'm sorry. I wouldn't have said we'd take the kid along if I'd thought you'd mind ...' he whispered as he held her close.

It was impossible not to return his kisses, not to catch fire from his ardent mouth, not to murmur that it didn't matter, and she was sorry she had been so silly about it and she quite understood.

'There's my girl ...' Dennis murmured against her mouth. He sighed. 'I'd far rather stay here kissing you, honey, but maybe we'd better go and pick that brat up. After all, Mrs. Crampton is my bread and butter ...'

It did not take them long to reach the large stone house perched overlooking the distant valley. Creena sat in the car while Dennis ran indoors to fetch the 'brat.' The light from the hall fell on Ailsa as she came out of the front door, her hand tucked through Dennis's arm, as she stared adoringly up at him. She was a tall, well-built girl with a mass of ash-blonde hair swept up in an elaborate hair-do, she was wearing a crimson frock that was much too tight for her and had a slit up the side of the skirt. Her eyes were darkened and her mouth a scarlet gash. just the way most young girls look when they were too eager to grow up—so it was all wrong for her to feel so smug and pompous, Creena decided. Ailsa was just a child playing at being grown-up—she should feel sorry for her.

But it was not easy to go on feeling sorry for anyone who was as rude and ruthless as Ailsa was. Creena was gasping with amazement and very conscious that Dennis was amused by Ailsa's brash talk, her affectations, her often crude expressions, her desire to make them think that she was accustomed to going to night clubs.

'Of course this will be all rather boring . . .' the young girl drawled. 'But it's better than sitting at home with Gran. She's in a real bate, tonight, Den—what happened?'

'Trouble at the hospital . . .' Dennis said curtly.

'Not again . . .' Ailsa sighed gustily. 'Really, poor Gran—you'd think people would be grateful to her for running the hospital not always giving her headaches. I suppose it was that awful Scotsman . . .'

'Scot . . .' Dennis corrected her and laughed. 'He prefers to be called a Scot . . .'

'That's not what Gran calls him . . .' Ailsa said, giving a squeal of laughter. 'She—'

Creena closed her eyes and tried to curl up in a ball, closing her ears at the same time. She thought of other things—of Dr. McGregor's kindness the time Norma had had mumps—his gentleness with Mike when Mike had hurt his heel on someone else's motor-bike—his humour when he had come to dinner and

19

taught Creena how to play chess. How was it Dennis and Dr. McGregor had never got on? Why had Dennis's voice held a triumphant note when he said that Dr. McGregor had gone?

It was a relief when they drew up outside the hotel and she and Ailsa hurried in to the cloakroom to leave their coats. Ailsa hardly spoke to her, devoting herself to her reflection in the mirror, adding more lipstick to her ugly mouth. Creena stood silently, her thoughts far away, half-wishing herself back at home instead of at the dance. And then Ailsa was ready and they went out into the crowded hall and Dennis was there, a tall sandy-haired man by his side whom Creena knew and liked— Bob Hamilton, who was in the police force.

'Nice to see you again, Creena,' Bob said, his grip hurting her hand as he smiled down at her. 'Could I have this dance?'

They could hear the band playing spirited music from the ballroom. Creena looked round to ask Dennis and saw that he had gone—he was leading Ailsa towards the dancing.

Trying to hide her dismay—for it was a rude way for Dennis to behave and unlike him— Creena smiled at Bob and went with him. But that first moment seemed to set the key to the whole evening. It was not that Creena went without partners—she hardly sat down the whole evening, but it was because Dennis had

20

taken her to the dance and only danced twice with her throughout the whole time. How could he treat her like that? Everyone must be talking about it. Why, Mrs. Isipin had paused by their table and smiled down at her, saying sweetly that she did hope dear Creena was enjoying herself, and how kind she was being to that dear child Ailsa, who was having a wonderful time.

Several times, Bob had glanced at her uneasily and asked if there was anything wrong. She had denied it strenuously and made a valiant effort to be gay and the life and soul of the party, but there had been a hollowness about her laughter that she was afraid others could hear.

Once, dancing with Dennis, she had ventured to say that she had a headache.

'Too bad . . .' he said. 'Haven't you any aspirin?'

So that was all the sympathy he had for her headache! Or did he guess it was a lie?

By three o'clock, the headache was no lie. Her head was throbbing painfully and her eyes smarting from the smoke-laden atmosphere. There were the four of them at the table — Dennis, Ailsa, Bob and herself.

'I think we should go,' Creena said. 'Ailsa's grandmother will be worrying.'

Ailsa's eyes were hostile. 'She won't worry. She trusts Dennis . . .' She turned to give him a brilliant smile. 'We needn't go yet, Dennis, need we? I'm having such fun.'

He hesitated. The ballroom was gradually emptying. He saw the band leader glancing at his watch. 'Just one more dance, Ailsa . . .' he said, standing up, holding out his arms.

Ailsa's eyes were shining. 'Heaven . . .' she said and went into his arms, resting her cheek against his, her eyes half-closed now, her face dreamy.

Bob stared after them and then turned to give Creena a quizzical smile.

'She's got it badly,' he said, laughing a little.

Creena was in the cloakroom putting on her coat when Ailsa joined her. Ailsa looked at her accusingly. 'Proper spoilsport . . .' she said, almost spitting the words out. 'What are you—jealous?' She watched the tell-tale colour rise in Creena's cheeks, and laughed. 'Well—maybe you are jealous and I don't blame you. Dennis likes me . . .' her voice lilted. 'He told me so . . . He doesn't love you, you know, Creena,' she went on, smiling, looking a little grotesque under the layers of make-up. 'He told me you were useful . . .'

Creena found a smile and nailed it to her face. 'Well, that's something, isn't it?' she said quietly. 'At least, I am useful.'

She walked into the hall to where Dennis was waiting impatiently, Ailsa close behind her. Creena made no move as Ailsa pushed past her to sit next to Dennis, holding his arm tightly, resting her head against it, looking up

22

at him and talking all the time in a shrill excited voice.

Creena sat as close to the door of the car as she could, almost welcoming the painful pressure of the door handle. She closed her eyes, her head throbbing. Was she jealous? Jealous of this stupid child? Had she grown to love Dennis —to become so possessive of him that she resented any other girl coming between them? And could Dennis be in love with this girl? Or . . .

She asked him when they had finally dropped Ailsa at her grandmother's house and they were alone in the car.

'In love with her?' Dennis sounded startled as he drove rapidly down the twisting road. 'Are you mad, honey? I was just being nice to her because she—or rather, her granny, is my bread and butter.'

Creena's throat was dry. 'She thinks you're in love with her.'

'That's a joke . . .' he said but he sounded annoyed. It was some miles later that he asked her abruptly: 'Are you jealous?'

Startled she looked up at him. 'Of course not,' she said quickly. Too quickly?

'Look,' Dennis's voice was icily-cold. 'If there's one thing I can't tolerate it is a jealous woman—or a possessive one. What right—'

Anger rose in her at the injustice of this. 'Dennis—you were . . . you were very rude to me tonight. In front of everyone . . . neglecting me and—'

'My . . .' He swore softly. 'Look—what right have you to say I neglected you? I took you there—I paid for the tickets, didn't I? And the drinks? And asked your old boyfriend Bob along to keep you happy? What right have you to say I was rude.'

'You took me and—'

'Sure I did—and then I had to take Ailsa along for business reasons. Look . . .' She could hear the anger in his voice. 'Look,' he went on. 'Have I ever given you any reason to believe that you own me? That you have a right to criticize me—lay down the law? You're right—I haven't. I know you're playing it your way—I know you let everyone think were going to be married but don't forget one thing . . .' His voice rose furiously. 'I've not proposed to you, yet, have I?'

She was watching the winding blinding streak of light ahead of them, giving glimpses of trees, of drops down the mountain side—his voice an angry blur in her ears. 'Dennis!' she cried out. 'Please don't drive so fast . . .'

'I'll drive as fast as I like . . .' he yelled at her. 'I'll—'

And then suddenly the white short poles were there in front of them—there was the scream of brakes—the skidding slithering of the car over the road and then a terrible noise—a fierce jolting that seemed to knock the breath out of her and then . . . Darkness.

24

CHAPTER TWO

When Creena opened her eyes, she was still in darkness. She moved her head restlessly and instantly a cool hand was on her wrist and a familiar voice said quietly, 'Everything is all right, Creena, just don't move. I'll get Doctor . . .'

Creena recognized Janice Hames's voice, a Sister at the hospital. Creena knew her well for they had often gone riding together over the mountains.

'Why is everything so dark . . .' Creena began in a whisper, but then she felt her hand taken in a warm one—surprisingly gentle fingers on her wrist, and a strange masculine voice saying: You have nothing to worry about, Miss Hall . . . Your face was cut close to your eyes . . . you are not blind . . . you will not be scarred.'

Was there amusement in his voice?

'Where am I—' she began and then corrected herself. 'I suppose this is the hospital? Why—'

'You were involved in an accident and—'

She remembered everything. Vividly. The horror of that terrible moment when she knew they were in big trouble—that terrible second as the car skidded. She remembered it all.

'Dennis?' she gasped as fear flooded her.

'Dr. Tyson is quite all right. Badly bruised his ribs—shock, of course . . . and he has broken his right arm. Apart from that, he is in perfect condition.'

Was there again a strange ironical note in his voice? Who was he, anyhow? That wasn't Dr. Pipp and if Dennis was in bed . . .

She tried to marshall her thoughts but it was an awful effort. Tried to imagine Dennis with a broken arm. How cross he would be—how he would hate to be helpless. Was he in great pain? She moved carefully. She felt stiff and very uncomfortable but there seemed to be nothing hurt. And then she began to remember more—the last quarrel—Dennis's ugly angry words . . . She shivered . . .

Again that warm friendly yet somehow impersonal hand was on her wrist.

'You escaped with slight concussion . . .' the deep voice told her, 'and considerable bruising and shock, naturally.'

'How long have I been unconscious?' she asked.

'Three days.'

Three days . . . The world seemed to spin round her.

'Dr. Tyson is naturally extremely upset . . .' the deep vibrant voice continued. 'He is eager to see you . . .'

'No . . . no . . .' Creena gasped. Suddenly she knew she could not bear Dennis near her. Those had been cruel unforgivable words he

26

had used. 'I won't see him . . .' She heard her voice rising hysterically.

'Then you shan't see him,' the deep calm voice told her. The next moment, she felt a slight prick in her arm and slowly, gradually, a blessed sleepiness filled her.

The next time she opened her eyes, she heard another voice she recognized. It was the husky glamorous voice of Elena Cartwright. She lived alone in a very big house on the Mount, the wealthy widow of a local millionaire.

'Oh, Doctor darling . . .' She was saying, in that husky seductive voice that was so effective with men. 'I really am bored to tears. Can't you put me in a room with something more lively? Poor Creena just moans and groans and—'

'She is heavily drugged . . .' the unknown doctor's voice held the now familiar note of irony.

'But it is such a bind lying here and listening . . . and when she comes round, I suppose she'll want to tell me all about her quarrel with Dennis . . .' the husky voice continued. 'I don't wonder Dennis got fed-up . . . she was always chasing him . . .' Listening, Creena stiffened with angry shock. Was that what everyone said? Elena Cartwright laughed softly. 'Not that I blame her . . . Dennis has something that definitely appeals to every woman . . . but then so have you, Doctor darling . . .' Her voice was

27

like a caress.

Creena drew a long careful breath. Elena was certainly what might be called a fast worker. How long could this unknown doctor have been here? Two days?

'Poor Dennis . . .' Elena went on. 'He is really suffering from a bad conscience. I saw him yesterday and he says he can't forgive himself for the things he said . . . Foolish boy —doesn't he realize that Creena would forgive him anything?'

Creena's hands clenched and unclenched slowly and the sharp tears stung her eyes.

'Anyhow, Doctor darling, be a lamb and have pity on me,' Elena went on almost gaily. 'Put me in a room with someone cheerful . . . after all I'm not really ill, am I?'

'Certainly not . . .' the unknown doctor sounded amused. 'You are in purely for observation purposes and in a few days you could go home, I think, and just come in to see us until all the tests are finished.'

'This allergy is really pretty ghastly, you know . . .' Elena said, her voice pathetic. 'It makes one frightfully edgy . . . I do wish—'

'You could be moved?' the doctor asked, his voice kind. 'Well, I'll speak to Matron and see what can be arranged.' There was the scraping sound of a chair moving as if he was standing up. Creena lay very still, composing her face, trying to look as if she was sound asleep. It must have been a convincing performance for

28

in a few moments she heard his footsteps go away. She had no idea if there were screens round her bed—or if Elena's cold critical eyes were watching her. It was difficult to lie there, still, not letting the other woman know she was awake and had heard every word she felt so vulnerable, like a butterfly pinned to a specimen board.

It was a relief in a moment to hear a scuffling sound and then the faint click-clack of slippers on the polished floor and the soft coughing noise the door gave when it was swung to . . . that meant Elena Cartwright had gone visiting again. Dennis? She had always chased Dennis . . .

Chased Dennis? Creena caught her breath with dismay. That was what Elena had said of her . . . and that Dennis was conscience-stricken about the things he had said

They had been cruel . . .

Restlessly Creena turned her head from side to side, tentatively fingering the bandages, longing to pull them off and see the world clearly again.

What had he said?

Have I ever given you any reason to believe you own me? I know you're playing it your way—letting everyone think we're going to be married.

I've not proposed to you—yet . . .

How could he have said such cruel things? Such wicked lies . . .

29

But were they lies? Had she unwittingly allowed people to think they were going to marry one day? Hadn't she thought so herself? Hadn't her mother thought so? Her father? Was it her fault? Yet what had she done wrong? Simply gone out with him whenever he asked her . . . simply let everyone see that she liked him more than a little . . . *had* she chased him?

She felt sick with humiliation and shame . . . and now Dennis, to make it all worse, was going to tell her he loved her, simply because . . . because he was sorry for her . . .

She must have dozed for when she awoke, the little ward was very quiet. Her mouth was horribly dry—her hand fumbled for and found the bell and pushed the button. In a moment, Janice was by her side, talking quietly, cheerfully.

'How are you feeling, Creena? Like a drink?'

'Oh, I would . . .' Creena hesitated. 'Is . . . is Elena . . .'

'Still here?' Janice asked. She chuckled. 'No—the doctor moved her—at her request.'

'Oh . . .' Creena hesitated.

Janice was laughing softly. 'He's got a lovely sense of humour—the doctor,' she said quietly, lifting Creena, plumping up the pillows. 'He's moved the glamorous Elena and put her with'—she paused to chuckle again—'Mrs. Isipin.'

Creena wanted to laugh. 'Oh, but . . . but perhaps he didn't know . . .'

Janice went on chuckling. 'What? How could he be in this small dorp forty-eight hours without knowing that Mrs. Isipin and Elena Cartwright are at daggers drawn?'

'What's wrong with Mrs. Isipin?'

'Fell and sprained her ankle in Miller Street . . . they think it may be more than a strain and she made so much fuss that, as we had a spare bed, it was easier to let her come here for a couple of nights. All is grist to the mill,' Janice added a little bitterly. 'And Mrs. Isipin can afford to pay.'

'This new doctor,' Creena asked later as she sipped the very welcome hot cup of tea.

'A friend of Dennis's,' Janice told her, an odd note in her voice. 'Seems they met when last Dennis was on holiday and when we found Dennis had a broken arm and was temporarily out of the picture . . . Oh, did you know Dr. McGregor walked out?' Janice asked, her voice changing again. It was odd how important tones became when you could not see. Janice was obviously very angry with Dr. McGregor . . . but then Janice had always been very much attracted by Dennis—something he had remarked on teasingly several times, boasting a little about it. Dr. McGregor and Dennis had never seen eye to eye. So she nodded and Janice went on: 'Your father came to help and so did Dr. Pipp—but they're both

31

too old to do this job full-time so Dennis wired to this doctor and he flew up next day.' Her voice changed: 'He is good, I must admit.' Her voice sounded flustered. 'Oh, I didn't see you there, sir. Our patient is conscious, Doctor Darling. Creena, this is . . .'

Creena stared into the heavy blackness, wondering what the doctor could be like. Fancy him letting patients and nurses be so familiar?

A warm firm hand held her wrist, a deep vibrant voice with laughter in it, said: 'Please do not look so shocked, Miss Hall. Sister was not being affectionate. My name happens to be Darling—Bartholomew Darling, but commonly known as Bart . . .'

Creena's face was red, she hoped he was not able to read her thoughts.

'You can imagine that the name has been a great source of annoyance to me in the past,' Dr. Darling went on, his voice amused. 'Especially at school where I had to fight almost continually because of it. However, I have now learned to accept it and it no longer worries me. It does, however, cause some strange thoughts in people's minds.'

She was flustered. 'When can I have the bandages off? I hate this . . .'

'I'm sure you do. A couple of days. You're not worrying? I assure you there will be no scars.'

'I'm not afraid of that,' Creena snapped,

moving restlessly. 'I just feel so . . . so helpless.'

'I know,' he said gently. 'Your parents are very anxious to see you. Do you feel equal to it?'

Creena hesitated. She could just imagine how her mother would flap—probably burst into floods of tears. Now if her father could come alone . . . but that would hurt her mother's feelings.

'Yes . . .' she said flatly.

The visit proved to be less of an ordeal than she had feared. Her mother's voice quavered a little as she spoke, she said that Creena could have been killed, that Dennis was to blame . . . but then Creena heard her father's deep reassuring voice as he said cheerfully that Creena was lucky to escape almost unscathed and that maybe it would teach Dennis a lesson not to drive so fast in future.

'If only he hadn't lost his temper . . . and his . . .' Creena's mother said.

Creena felt herself shiver. So the whole world knew that she and Dennis had quarrelled? That he had lost his temper . . . Had he also told everyone what he had said to her?

'I think we've been here long enough for the first visit,' Creena heard her father say firmly. 'Come along, my dear . . .'

His mouth brushed hers lightly. 'You're doing fine, darling . . .' he said softly.

After they had gone, Creena lay for a long

time alone and then she found herself caught up in the usual routine of hospital life, and the days slipped by, with Dr. Darling visiting her regularly, never again suggesting that she see Dennis. At visiting hours, someone or other visited Creena but were never allowed to stay long. Mike popped in to tell her how the horses were but seemed ill-at-ease and almost delighted when the bell rang to say visiting time was over, Norma came with flowers from the garden and wanted to know if Creena didn't think she was being very unkind to poor Dennis.

'He really is upset, Creena . . .' she said earnestly. 'I've seen him and he is awfully unhappy because you won't see him . . .'

Creena's mouth tightened. 'It's my business,' she said rudely.

'Well, really, Creena . . .' her sister sounded disgusted. 'I always thought you were a Christian . . .'

Creena tried not to smile. 'What has that to do with it?'

Norma's young voice was disapproving. 'They forgive . . .'

'It's not so easy to forget . . .'

'But Creena . . .' Norma persisted. 'Dennis says he had too much to drink—that he was on edge because of something Mrs. Crampton had said and . . . Honestly, haven't you ever said things you really don't mean and then regretted them later?'

34

Creena swallowed. If only they would leave her alone! 'I think Dennis did mean them,' she said quietly.

It was wonderful when Dr. Darling removed the bandages and she could see again. Curiously she stared at him. He was totally different from what she had expected. Somehow his voice had made her think of him as an older man but now she saw he was in his mid-thirties. A big man—tall, very broad-shouldered, he seemed to fill the small room. His deep blue eyes met her gaze.

'Well,' he said in that amused way he had, 'am I what you expected?'

Her face burned. 'I thought you'd be older . . .'

He straddled a chair by her side and smiled. She saw the laughter wrinkles round his eyes, the firm chin, the gentle mouth. 'Whatever made you think that?'

'I don't know . . .' She felt uneasy suddenly for his eyes never flickered. 'Your voice . . .'

'I am thirty-six . . . getting on . . .' he said teasingly.

There was something unusual about him. Hitherto, she had always thought Dennis the most impressive man she knew—his personality sometimes almost overpowering. But next to Bart Darling, Dennis would be like a shadow. Bart was taller, broader, and had a quiet deep strength that you could sense. You could not imagine Bart Darling sulking—he

35

would be above such behaviour. Nor cringing to Mrs. Crampton—even if his job depended on it.

Suddenly Creena remembered something Meg Gordon, who came daily to nurse at the hospital because she lived with an invalid mother who could not be left alone at night, had said: 'He's what I call a real doctor . . .' she had said her voice earnest. To Creena, listening in her strange frightening darkness, there had been a note of hero-worship in Meg's voice. But now Creena knew what Meg had meant. Somehow Bart Darling epitomized all the things you expected in a doctor—things Creena's father had . . . but that Dennis seemed to lack. A feeling of controlled strength, for instance. With Dennis, you had a feeling of strength but it was almost frightening for you never had a feeling that he could control it. He was a man of quick tempers, moods, sweet reconciliations. Somehow you could not imagine Bart Darling quarrelling with anyone—he would be too dignified . . .

Bart Darling smiled and held out a small mirror. 'You're a strange girl,' he drawled. 'Don't you want to see if your face is all right.'

'You told me it was,' Creena said and wondered why Bart gave her a strange look— almost a look of gratitude, she would have said had it not sounded absolute nonsense, for why should Bart be grateful for such a remark?

'You trust me?' he asked and there was a faintly ironic note in his voice.

'Of course,' she said simply, and realized that it was true.

All the same, it was good to look in the mirror and see that her face was unharmed, merely small white scars that could hardly be seen. She looked very pale and somehow thinner—interesting, perhaps? She stared at her reflection curiously, it wasn't a pretty face, she decided ruefully. Oval, it had a puckish look, with high cheekbones and slanting green eyes. If only she had long dark lashes, hers were so fair . . . if only . . .

'Satisfied?' Bart Darling teased.

Colouring self-consciously, Creena looked at him. 'I—'

He stood up slowly, towering above her. 'You're a very pretty girl . . .' he said almost casually, 'but I think you can be cruel . . .'

He was at the door before she got her breath back and found her voice.

'What do you mean?' she asked indignantly.

He leant against the door, staring down at her, his eyes narrowed.

'Don't you think it is cruel to refuse to see Dr. Tyson?'

Her cheeks burned. 'I think it is my business.'

Bart Darling folded his arms as if he had all the time in the world.

'It happens to be mine, too,' he drawled.

'Dr. Tyson is my patient and your refusal to see him is sadly retarding his progress . . .'

'That's ridiculous . . .'

His dark brows lifted. Strange how dark they were for his thick hair was light brown. 'I beg your pardon?' he drawled.

She blushed again. 'I didn't mean to be rude but . . but . . .'

He came back to the bedside and sat down. 'Well, you were rude,' he said flatly.

She felt worse than ever. 'I'm—I'm sorry.' Why, the wretched man had put her in the wrong—made her feel guilty.

'Look . . .' he said quietly, his deep voice seeming to fill the small room. 'Dennis Tyson is suffering from shock—his arm is very painful and not healing well . . . he isn't sleeping well, either. He feels very guilty because of his behaviour. He hasn't done anything criminal . . . anyone can be careless and have an accident.'

She pleated folds in the sheet, not looking at him. 'Oh—that . . .' she said casually. 'That didn't matter . . . it was . . .'

'The quarrel?' Bart asked quietly.

She looked at him swiftly and met his thoughtful gaze. She nodded.

He went on: 'In a quarrel one often says things one does not mean. Is it just to condemn him unheard?'

'You don't understand . . .' Creena said miserably. 'I can't . . .'

38

'Look—I am your doctor,' Ban Darling said. Suddenly he took hold of her hand, holding it tightly between his hands. 'Anything you say is between us. What unforgivable things could Dennis Tyson have said to you?'

Her mouth was dry—she looked everywhere but each time, his eyes seemed to draw hers back to his, like a magnet. She swallowed. 'He said . . . he said I was chasing him—that I had led everyone to believe we were to be married . . . that he . . . he hadn't proposed . . .'

Just saying the awful words seemed to make it worse. To her utter amazement, she saw that Bart Darling was not shocked.

'So you feel he jilted you?'

She swallowed again. 'He insulted me . . . I didn't . . . didn't ever chase him.'

Bart smiled outright. 'Then you must be the only girl in the town who didn't . . . judging from the local grapevine. Don't you think, Creena . . .' he went on, and she realized that he had used her Christian name unconsciously, '. . . that perhaps Dennis Tyson was scared? Have you ever thought of the difference between a man's and a girl's outlook on life? To a girl, marriage is usually her goal—she is made for marriage and motherhood and everything in her way of life leads slowly to that wonderful wedding-day. To a man, it often means loss . . . loss of freedom, of financial independence for he is assuming great responsibilities, it may mean cancelling

39

some of his ambitions, curbing his plans. A man gives up a great deal when he marries . . .'

She tried to wrench her hand free but he held it tightly. Her cheeks were blazing.

'I take it you have never married?'

He looked at her thoughtfully. 'No. You see, I have never been in love,' he said.

CHAPTER THREE

They say it is the gentle answer that turneth away wrath, Creena thought half an hour later when Dr. Darling had left her and she was alone, grateful that she had no one sharing her bright little ward, glad of the chance to think over the things he had said.

She closed her eyes, seeing again the handsome, impressive face and the way he had looked at her, almost sadly, as he had said simply that he had never been in love. It made her wonder about his life. A handsome man of thirty-six who has never been in love was surely something to wonder at. In another man—or a man of a different character, it might have been a naive sort of remark—it could have been a *line*. But she knew that Bart Darling had spoken the truth.

Had he always been so dedicated to his work? Had he perhaps been poor and had to struggle to become a doctor? Yet that would not have stopped him from falling in love ...

The perpetual crying and chattering from the African wards made a rather mournful background to her thoughts. Could Bart Darling be right? Could she have frightened Dennis by her behaviour? Was she blaming him from lack of thought on her part—taking it for granted he was wrong? Had she perhaps seemed possessive? She knew he was a very ambitious man—she knew that he was an orphan, that he had no financial background to fall back on. She knew he wanted to specialize one day—that it was going to take all his time and cost a great deal of money. Was he, perhaps, afraid of marriage for that reason? Because it would put paid to his ambitions?

Of course Bart Darling was so right in one thing—it was every girl's dream. To fall in love with the right man, to marry, have a home and children. It was funny but she had never thought of it before from the man's side— never realized what a man must give up. Not only his freedom but his independence, his chance of forging ahead in his career, perhaps . . .

The days passed slowly and gradually she was allowed to get up—to go to the bathroom—walk down the corridor and gaze out of the wide windows at the sun-lit scene. She would watch the small African children playing in the dust as their mothers sat round stolidly, chatting to one another, waiting for their turn to go into out-patients. The day she was leaving the hospital, Creena seized a moment when Dr. Darling was alone in her small ward.

'I . . . I've decided to see Dennis,' she said bluntly.

He had been examining her chart—he looked up quickly, a strange expression on his face. 'I'm glad,' he said. 'I don't think you'll regret it.'

It was absurd but it took all her courage to dress and then walk down the corridor to the ward Dennis was in. Most of the ward doors were open and Creena was very conscious of curious eyes as she passed them. It was awful—like being a goldfish in a bowl. Everyone knew they had quarrelled—everyone knew why—and now everyone would know that she was going to see Dennis. It was just as Elena Cartwright had said . . . and yet it was different. She was going to see Dennis because Bart had told her that Dennis's health would improve if she did—because Bart had shown her Dennis's side of it . . . but she was not going to see Dennis because she wanted to go back to where they had been before the quarrel. Her feelings for Dennis had completely changed.

The door was half-open—she knocked lightly and then went in. Bart had said he would tell Dennis she was coming to see him.

'Darling!' Dennis cried out exultantly. She stared at the dark-haired handsome man sitting up in bed, propped by pillows, his arm at an awkward angle in a cast. His dark face was radiant—he held out his good hand. 'This is wonderful of you, darling . . .'

She gave him her hand and then found he would not let it go. She had to pull the chair close to the bed as a result. He gazed at her hungrily.

'Bless you, Creena . . .' he said. 'You don't know how this will help me—knowing you've forgiven me.' He gave her no chance to reply, lifting her hand to his lips for a moment and then going on. 'You are wonderful, darling. How could I be so terribly rude—so cruel . . . how could I have . . . Oh, darling, I could have killed you . . .'

She smiled but her face felt stiff. She was horribly aware that Dennis was speaking loudly—that his words would echo all down the corridor.

'It was an accident,' she said.

'Accident!' Dennis almost exploded. 'It was my abominable carelessness—there is no excuse. I lost my temper and my control. I'm sorry, darling.' His voice was charged with an unusual humility. Again he kissed her hand passionately. 'And you've forgiven me?' he went on eagerly. 'We'll behave just as if it had never happened?'

She hesitated. Things were no longer the

same. She looked at him with cool detached eyes—knowing that he was acting. That he might have meant some of the things he had said but mostly, he was playing to an audience. For some reason, he wanted her forgiveness.

'Did Mrs. Crampton come to see you?' Dennis went on, his face changing. 'She came and tore a number of strips off me . . .' he said ruefully. 'She was angry about Ailsa . . .'

'Ailsa?' Creena echoed.

Dennis nodded. 'You were right, darling, quite right,' he said with this strange new humility she could not understand. 'We kept Ailsa out too late . . . her grandmother was furious with me. She also said that everyone was talking about the way I behaved at the dance—and that Ailsa made a spectacle of herself.'

'But . . . but Mrs. Crampton wasn't at the dance . . .'

'Exactly . . .' Dennis gave a bitter laugh. 'Someone took it on themselves to tell her. Easy to guess who it was. The same woman who was sent in here with a sprained ankle because her poor husband was so delighted to get rid of her for a few days . . .'

'Dennis!' Creena gasped, shocked. She tore her hand free and went to close the door, turning, leaning against it, staring at him in dismay. 'Mrs. Isipin is just down the corridor . . . she might have heard.'

'I hope she did . . . the old . . . old besom . . .'

44

Dennis said viciously.

'But Dennis, are you sure it was Mrs. Isipin?'

'Who else? She hates me . . . I don't know why . . .'

'I think she hates most people . . .' Creena said thoughtfully. 'Poor thing.'

'Ha!' Dennis snorted. 'Spare your pity for me and the poor kid. Mrs. Crampton promptly packed Ailsa off to some expensive finishing school in Switzerland.'

Creena had to move as the door handle was turned and the door hit her back. Janice Hames stood in the doorway, her eyes intent on Dennis. A tall stately girl, her prematurely-white hair gave her an ethereal look.

'Your father has come for you, Creena . . .' she said, her voice flat.

Creena was going when she remembered something. 'Oh, Dennis—how is your arm?'

He grimaced and smiled at Janice. 'Not too good, is it, Sister? Our new doctor seems slightly worried. By the way, darling, what do you think of Bartholomew . . .' The way he said the name caricatured it, Creena thought. So Dennis didn't like Dr. Darling!

'He seems very competent,' she said a little primly.

Dennis shouted with laughter. 'Hark at her. What do you think of him, Sister Hames?' he demanded.

'I agree with Creena . . .' Janice said with

45

equal demureness. 'He is a very competent and dedicated doctor . . .'

'But what do you think of him as a man?' Dennis demanded, his eyes alight with mischief. 'You should watch Meg's face when he passes by—a bad case of hero-worship, I'd say . . .'

Creena escaped quickly, angry with Dennis for behaving so. Surely he knew that was how Janice Hames looked at him? As if she was prepared to be the cloak Sir Walter Raleigh threw across a puddle for Queen Elizabeth. She collected her small night case and hurried out of the hospital, almost throwing herself in her father's arms as he came to meet her.

'It's wonderful to be out of that place . . .' she said, sitting by his side in the big shabby car as they wended their way along the tree-lined roads.

Her father gave her a quick concerned glance. 'Getting you down?'

She moved her hands restlessly, folding her pink shirtwaister into folds with nervous fingers. 'Dad—they're so inquisitive and . . . and Dennis would speak so loudly—the whole town knows . . .'

'You saw Dennis?' her father's voice was devoid of expression. 'I thought you refused to see him.'

'I did but Bart . . . I mean Dr. Darling . . .'

They slowed up to let a herd of cattle stray across the road, followed by a small native boy

46

with a stick bigger than himself.

'Advised you to?' her father asked, sounding surprised.

Creena told him of her conversation. 'He said that Dennis's progress was being retarded—that he felt guilty . . . He didn't strike me that way.'

Her father grunted. 'Dennis isn't the conscience-stricken type.'

Creena repeated the whole conversation—merely leaving out the part where Dr. Darling had said he had never been in love. Somehow that seemed to be a confidence—a secret between them.

'I think perhaps Dr. Darling is right, Daddy. I hadn't realized before what a man gives up when he gets married.'

'A man in love thinks it is worth it . . .' her father said dryly.

'But Dennis is very ambitious . . .'

'And ruthless. Don't worry, Creena. If marriage to you would harm Dennis's career, he would not want to marry you.'

'But I don't think he does . . .'

'Then why the great reconciliation scene?' her father asked.

Creena sighed. 'I don't know . . . I just don't know. You've met Dr. Darling, of course, Dad?'

'I've assisted him at several operations. He's working under very difficult conditions. The hospital badly needs another full-time doctor.'

They were crossing the narrow bridge, swinging round the corner, climbing the mountain towards their home. The warm sunshine caressed her cheeks—a slight breeze tugged at her hair. It was good to be going home.

'Do you like him, Dad?'

Her father nodded slowly. 'I hardly know him, of course, but he strikes me as being a very good man.' He half-smiled. 'I believe he is already doing battle with the Matron . . . and she, poor soul, without Dennis to back her up, is caught betwixt two poles—Darling's righteous wrath and Mrs. Crampton's fury.'

Creena thought of the Matron—a plump elderly woman who was quite unable to make a decision. The last person to be in the charge of a hospital but as her father had always said, Matron was a very good 'yes-woman' and that was all Mrs. Crampton required. He had always disliked working at a private hospital, he had said; particularly disliking Mrs. Crampton's methods of keeping a very restraining hand on expenses.

'What's the trouble now?' Creena asked. They were nearing the paddock—she leaned forward eagerly—looking for the horses.

'Usual—short supply of necessary drugs . . . orders to cut down on the milk for the African children . . . Darling doesn't go for that sort of behaviour . . .'

'What does Mrs. Crampton say?'

Her father laughed. 'No one knows. I have heard she said that it was only a temporary appointment.'

A strange desolation filled Creena. 'Is he here?'

'As a locum for Dennis . . .' her father said, slowing the car up to take the steep turn over the cattle trap.

Creena's mother came hurrying down the winding stone steps, flinging her arms round Creena, talking eagerly. Once indoors, she turned to Creena, her face expectant.

'You've made it up with Dennis,'

It was a statement and not a question. Creena stared at her in dismay.

'Who told you?'

Her mother coloured, ran an agitated hand through her hair. 'Oh dear, darling, I shouldn't have let it out. Mrs. Hunter who mends the linen at the hospital telephoned me. She knew I'd be glad to hear that you and Dennis are—'

'Are what, Mother?' Creena asked very coldly.

Her mother looked startled; her eyes flicking away quickly.

'Why—why, good friends, of course, darling. What else?' she said hastily and murmuring something about telling Violet what they were having for lunch, hurriedly left the room.

Creena sat down on the edge of her divan heavily. If only people would mind their own business. Leave her alone. She looked round

49

the pretty little room and realized she had still not escaped from the goldfish bowl. She unpacked her case, opening her window wider, touching the soft white net frilly curtains, straightening the deep-pink bedspread.

She went out into the garden and joined her father on the swing chair. He was reading a copy of *The Lancet* but put it down, adjusting the canopy so that the sun was not in her eyes.

'Now what's wrong?' he asked gently.

Creena looked at him, her deep-set green eyes unhappy. 'Dad—why does Mummy keep thrusting Dennis down my throat?'

He smiled ruefully. 'Because she wants you to be happy.'

'Does she think Dennis could make me happy?'

He shrugged his shoulders. 'Your mother is a romanticist, Creena. She believes that wedding bells inevitably mean that happiness will follow. Dennis is the best-looking, most popular, eligible young man in the neighbourhood. She wants you to have the best—and to her mind, Dennis is the best.'

'As simple as that,' Creena said, pulling a face.

Her father chuckled. 'To her eyes, it is. But don't worry, love, no one can make you marry Dennis if you don't love him.'

Suddenly she was frightened. Suddenly she felt as if all the forces in the world were converging on her—forcing her into Dennis's arms. She felt trapped. 'Dad—I wish we didn't live here,' she said almost desperately. 'I wish we lived in a big city where no one knew us . . .'

He chuckled but she saw that he understood. 'You'd still have your mother's romantic nature to contend with, Creena,' he said. 'It's in your hands, child. If you don't love Dennis, just steer clear of him. Refuse his invitations . . .' He looked at her sharply. 'You don't love Dennis, do you?'

Creena narrowed her eyes, staring at the lovely mountain view—the blue cloudless sky—the winding silver ribbon of a river far below.

'No . . . I don't love him . . .' she said slowly. 'I like him —I enjoy being with him but . . .'

The distant sound of the gong summoned them for lunch. Her father stood up, smiling down at her. 'Creena child, remember—so long as there is a *but* in your thoughts, it isn't love . . .'

CHAPTER FOUR

Oh, it was good to be home again, Creena thought, as she wandered round the four-acre grounds, taking cabbages to her mother's hens, going into the paddock to talk to and fondle the horses, or just sitting on the swing-chair, gazing at the wonderful view of the mountains.

Although she was supposed to be perfectly fit, her father had urged her not to hurry things. She had received a nasty shock, he kept saying.

How right he was, Creena thought, swinging the chair a little, the small dachshund curled up on her lap as she gently tugged at his silky ears. It had been the revelation of a new Dennis—a different Dennis from the man she had liked so much. It wasn't only the words he had used—the accusation that she had been chasing him . . . somehow what shocked her much more was the fact that when she had begged him to drive more slowly, he had deliberately accelerated. Almost as if . . . as if he had wanted to make her frightened, wanted her to be punished for some crime she might have unwittingly committed. If he truly loved her . . .

But somehow she could not imagine Dennis loving anyone but—Dennis. She leaned down and pulled a blade of grass from the lawn and sucked it thoughtfully. Maybe she had got Dennis on the brain, maybe she was making a molehill out of a mountain . . . suddenly she was laughing, amused at her own dreamy folly. Why, what she meant was a mountain out of a molehill. Dennis liked her, found her good fun; it suited him to have a girl to take out, a girl well-trained in a doctor's forcedly difficult social life, a girl understanding that he must often be late, must often postpone outings at the last moment. She was useful to him—

convenient. It was just other people who read more into their relationship than there actually was.

She heard the tooting of a car horn long before the car turned in over the cattle trap below. In a moment, Creena was on her feet, tumbling the little dog gently to the ground, smoothing out her green shirt-waister where the dog's body had crumpled it, and then she was running down the narrow winding pathway of stones to the flat parking ground below under the wattle trees.

'Audrey,' Creena cried excitedly.

The car had stopped, the door opened and out tumbled a short slight girl with an elfin face and an Italian bob of dark silky hair.

'Creena,' she cried with equal excitement. 'What's all this I hear? Dennis trying to kill you after a frightful row—and some new doctor come to live here . . .'

Audrey was her best friend and Creena was delighted to see her back from her trip overseas to England and Europe. Arm in arm they climbed the steps, laughing as they nearly pushed one another over, both talking excitedly. Perched on the swing chair, they exchanged news eagerly, Creena asking about Audrey's new boy friends and seeing her friend's dramatic little face sadden as she shook her head.

'Not one worth losing a night's sleep over, Creena. I'm afraid the trip didn't work . . . I'm

53

just not cured . . .' For a moment, Creena was afraid Audrey was going to cry, but the next moment Audrey was laughing. Creena was the only one to know that Audrey was deeply in love with a married man who lived in Johannesburg and that she was trying to cure herself of what she hoped was only an infatuation. 'But tell me about you—did Dennis really crash the car deliberately?' Audrey demanded, her dark eyes flashing.

'Of course not . . .' Creena cried in dismay. 'The things that get distorted here. I'll tell you what actually happened . . .'

After she had told the story, Audrey rocked herself backwards and forwards, clutching her knees, her shapely legs showing to advantage in the yellow jeans.

'All the same, Dennis shouldn't have behaved like that with Ailsa,' Audrey said, discounting Creena's generous attempt to absolve Dennis from blame. 'It was very rude indeed—I don't wonder you were mad with him. But then we all know Dennis has the manners of a pig—except when it pays him to be polite. How could he have said such beastly things to you, Creena? Just a pack of lies.'

'I haven't chased him, have I?' Creena asked unhappily.

Audrey turned to her at once. 'Of course you haven't. Don't be a mug, Creena. Dennis has done all the chasing, if any chasing was done. I mean, you've known one another for several years, have gone out together a lot . . . after all, Dennis needn't have asked you out at all, need he? No, he was just mad about something and so he wanted a whipping boy and you happened to be convenient.'

Creena traced the pattern on the cushions of the swing chair. 'He did tell me that when he took Ailsa indoors, Mrs. Crampton was waiting in her dressing-gown . . .' Creena could not help chuckling. 'He said she looked the funniest sight on earth—you know how short and fat she is . . . well, she had an enormous quilted purple . . . yes, purple . . . dressing-gown on, and her hair was done up in multicoloured rollers and her face covered with cream. But he said she might have had a rolling pin in her hand from the way she berated him . . .'

'He always was scared of Mrs. Crampton,' Audrey said contemptuously.

'You don't like Dennis, do you?' Creena said abruptly.

She watched the colour flood Audrey's cheeks but her friend's eyes met hers squarely. 'No, I think he's out for all he can get and he just doesn't care who gets hurt on the way . . .'

Thinking back into the dim past, Creena remembered something she had heard about Dennis and Audrey years before, when Creena was away at boarding school. It was very vague and hard to recall—but she could dimly hear Mrs. Isipin's sarcastic voice saying that for once Dennis Tyson had bitten off more than he could chew and that Audrey Hamilton had sent him running with his tail between his legs.

'You knew Dennis before I did . . .' Creena said, trying to remember the details.

Audrey gave her a rueful smile. 'Yes—I did. We went out several times and then we decided we just weren't one another's type. You're not jealous?'

It was Creena's turn to blush. 'Of course not,' she said hastily. 'Besides I'm not in love with Dennis . . .'

'Aren't you?' Audrey's eyes were shrewd. 'Are you sure you are not? Would you be so hurt and shocked by his words if you didn't love him?'

Creena caught her breath with dismay. 'Oh, Audrey . . . I hope I'm not—'

'Creena! Creena!' Her mother was calling.

'We're here, Ma!' Creena shouted back. 'Audrey's here.'

Mrs. Hall was panting a little as she climbed the steep grassy slope to the swing-chair. She beamed at the two girls. 'How nice to see you back, Audrey. Did you have a wonderful time?'

'Yes, thank you, Mrs. Hall . . .' Audrey smiled back.

Mrs. Hall turned to Creena. 'Dennis is on the telephone, dear . . . It's urgent, he says . . .' she added as she saw the indecision on her daughter's face. 'You'll stay for tea, Audrey?'

'Thanks, I'd love to. Creena and I have so much to talk about.'

They walked down the lawn together, Creena absurdly reluctant to speak to Dennis on the telephone. Why must he call her every day? Why send her flowers as he did? It was making people talk and that seemed so strange and unlike him, for hitherto, he had been so scrupulously careful that they were formal at the hospital and never let their friendship be taken too seriously. Now he was doing the exact opposite—he seemed to want to shout it from the housetops . . and she didn't want to, for she had this strange frightening sensation of being rushed into something she feared.

'Darling . . .' Dennis's voice was warm in her ear. 'I've rung up to say good-bye. I'm being sent to Jo'burg to have this arm of mine reset.' His voice was bitter. 'Seems that old fool of a Pipp set it badly and things are not healing as they should. It would have to be my right arm, of course. I'd hate to have to give up surgery.'

Creena's quick sympathy was caught. 'Oh, I am sorry, Dennis. I do hope they can put it right. It must be so worrying for you.'

His sigh echoed in her car. 'You're right, darling. Thanks be, I have you.' He hurried on before she could say anything. 'You won't forget me, Creena? I'll write to you every day, darling . . .'

Even as she answered him, she had the strangest sensation that Dennis was acting a part, that he was saying those loving words for an audience to hear. Yet why? It just didn't make sense.

At last she managed to end the conversation. 'The best of luck, Dennis.'

As she hurried out to the stoep where her mother was pouring out tea and chatting to Audrey, Creena came into the tail end of a sentence.

'. . . . natural, of course, for her to resent Dennis behaving in such a stupid fashion, but he didn't mean what he said, of course. He was just angry . . .'

'Then he's old enough to be able to control his anger,' Creena said quickly, her cheeks burning as she faced her mother. 'You've always scolded us for saying unkind things when we're mad. You've always said that the relief saying those unkind things gives one, just isn't worth while because of the pain they cause and the lasting damage they may do . . .'

Mrs. Hall looked startled. 'Yes, you are right, Creena, I have always said that. Maybe it's different for a man. A young man. I think he resented the way Mrs. Crampton had spoken to him . . .'

'She was cracking the whip,' Audrey put in.

Her two companions stared at her. Audrey smiled at them and passed the plate of crisp tartlets to Creena. 'Be honest, Creena, and admit the truth. Dennis is an ambitious man— he is thinking of the future. Mrs. Crampton

58

can help him quite a lot.' As if she sensed Mrs. Hall's displeasure at such a frank remark, Audrey changed the subject. 'By the way— what is this new doctor like. Everyone calls him the darling doctor.'

Creena began to laugh. Rudi was nibbling her ankles gently, nudging her until she surreptitiously slipped him a piece of her tart. 'His name is Bartholomew Darling and the first time I heard someone call him Doctor Darling, I nearly fell off the bed. It was at the hospital and it was Elena Cartwright.' She smiled as Audrey whistled softly. 'Yes, in her most seductive voice. I thought well, well, who's this new admirer and then I heard the nurses calling him it and when I met him, I knew no one would be likely to call him doctor darling like that and get away with it.'

'Why? What's he like? Stodgy?'

'Very dignified. He's older than Dennis—a very big impressive sort of man,' Creena said thoughtfully. 'Very fair hair which needs cutting . . . very blue eyes, a deep vibrating sort of voice. I'd say he would be a very good doctor.'

'Good?'

'Well . . . sort of dedicated, if you know what I mean. Like . . . like Dad.'

Audrey looked thoughtful. 'I understand Dennis sent for him?'

'Yes, Dr. McGregor had left suddenly and Dennis was injured and Dr. Pipp and Dad

59

couldn't carry on alone, he wired to Dr. Darling. Apparently they met when Dennis was on holiday and Dr. Darling was interested in a post up here.'

'Do you like him, Mrs. Hall?' Audrey asked abruptly, turning to face her hostess.

Creena's mother hesitated. 'I think I agree with Creena—he is a very dedicated man. I'm not sure if I like him or not . . .'

'But, Ma . . .' Creena cried in amazement, 'there just isn't anything about him you couldn't like . . .'

The telephone bell shrilling sent Mrs. Hall inside the thatched house and the two girls wandered down to the car.

'Give me a lift down to the Market, Audrey,' Creena said, grabbing a shopping basket as they walked through the kitchen. 'I promised Mum that I'd go and get some things. Dad is up at the hospital and I can 'phone him from there to pick me up.'

Sitting side by side in the car, Audrey wanted to know more about Dr. Darling. 'It's like a wave of excitement going through the dorp,' she said, laughing. 'I've only been back two days and everyone—but everyone—is talking about him. I've heard so many different things. That he is terribly handsome—that he is quite plain—that he is frightfully interesting and that he hardly opens his mouth.' She laughed again. 'I'm just dying to meet him.'

'He's single,' Creena said. 'Maybe you will

60

be his type.'

'Me?' Audrey grimaced in horror. 'No thanks, Creena. I'm not the doctor's wife type. When I marry, I want to come first in my husband's life . . .' Her happy face clouded for a second. 'When I marry,' she said bitterly. 'I doubt if I ever will.'

Creena met Mrs. Isipin as she wandered round the colourful market where the African women squatted on the ground or on wooden boxes, their wares spread out before them on newspaper. Creena had bought vegetables and paw-paws, oranges and bananas when a voice hailed her.

'Creena—and how are you these days?'

Creena swung round, startled and a little dismayed. Mrs. Isipin had a tongue that was dipped in acid. Now Creena saw that the dark eyes were glinting maliciously and with a sinking of her heart, Creena remembered the stupid way Dennis had talked about Mrs. Isipin in a loud voice, at the hospital, when Creena had gone to see him.

Mrs. Isipin was talking in her harsh parrot-like voice. 'I didn't see you before I left the hospital. Creena, Dr. Darling seemed to think it was wiser to keep you away from your friends. I hear that you and Dennis made up your quarrel.' Her eyes were like sharp spears, glinting. 'When are the wedding bells going to start pealing?'

Creena's cheeks were hot with anger.

61

'There has been no question—' she began stiffly.

Mrs. Isipin snorted with what was, perhaps, supposed to be amusement.

'Don't be so coy, Creena. Of course you and Dennis will eventually marry. You'll make him a good and useful wife and Mrs Crampton approves . . .' She cackled as she watched Creena's face go an even deeper red. 'I had left the hospital before you had that touching reconciliation scene,' Mrs. Isipin went on smoothly, 'but needless to say I heard all about it . . .'

Even in her helpless anger, Creena was conscious of relief. That meant Mrs. Isipin had gone before that last day—before Dennis's stupid unkind remark about 'someone's' husband sending her to hospital with a sprained ankle in order to get a bit of peace. The next moment Creena knew that she need not have worried. Dennis was careful of what he said—even though he disliked Mrs. Isipin, he would not willingly anger her. He knew the power her acid tongue had, knew the way she could injure an 'enemy.' Dennis was too clever.

'I see Audrey is back,' Mrs. Isipin went on. 'Has she managed to find a husband in Europe? Dear knows no man in his senses in this town would marry her. Extravagant little monkey that she is . . . a good thing her father is so wealthy but it's a pity he keeps marrying young women who can't handle Audrey. She needs a good spanking and—'

Creena could bear no more. 'Audrey is my friend, Mrs. Isipin,' she exploded suddenly. 'I'm meeting my father. Good-bye.' She turned blindly and rushed through the narrow aisles formed by the Africans who were calling out the names of their products. She bumped violently into a tall man and felt his warm hands on her bare elbows as he steadied her.

'Where's the fire?' he asked, in a deep voice.

Creena looked up into Bartholomew Darling's face. 'I'm sorry . . .' she gasped 'I . . . I guess I was rushing blindly because I was mad.'

One thick eyebrow was lifted. 'Not with me, I hope?'

Creena laughed. 'No, with Mrs. Isipin.' Her face flamed again. 'She says such—such beastly things . . .'

She found herself walking by his side, climbing the steep gravel road back to the main road. 'I know . . .' he said, his voice grim. 'I'm afraid she cannot help it. It would be interesting to know something of her past life—the reason for her hatred of mankind. Someone must have hurt her pretty badly.'

'She hurts plenty of others,' Creena said indignantly. How like a doctor! It was just the way her father talked. They never condemned anyone—could always hunt for a pathological reason.

'You should take it from whence it comes,' he told her. 'Not let it worry you.'

'Easy to talk . . .'

The doctor laughed suddenly.

'How right you are. It is easy to talk. I remember . . .' His voice changed. 'I was once in a situation in which people like Mrs. Isipin could do me untold damage. It puzzled me. They didn't hate me and yet they could not resist stirring up disapproval, criticism, hostility.' He sighed. 'I wonder what satisfaction such people get out of it.'

They paused on the main road. Cars were driving past them as the government offices released the civil servants. Africans were hurrying down the road, carrying bundles on their heads, babies on their backs. There was laughter and noise and dust. Dr Darling hesitated, looking at Creena's heavily laden basket.

'Can I run you home?'

'Could you?' Creena glanced at her wrist watch. 'I'll have missed Daddy by now. I meant to 'phone him at the hospital and ask him to pick me up.'

'My car's over here.' Dr. Darling led the way. It was a large black conservative-looking car.

As he drove her home, they chatted lightly. Creena glanced at him several times sideways, wondering if that broad-shouldered slow-moving man would be thought handsome by

Audrey. His face was by no means classical—his nose looked as if he had played a lot of rugger. He had a wide gentle sort of mouth, a friendly shy smile that reached his eyes. He had a thick stubborn-looking chin. He was . . . very impersonal.

As he left her at her gate, she realized the truth of this. No, he said very politely, he would not drop in for a drink or a cup of tea. He needed to get back to the hospital to see and check a patient he was operating on next day. He was glad to see her looking so well but advised her not to overdo things. And then he was gone. She climbed the steps to the front door feeling absurdly desolate. He had been very polite but . . . but he had treated her just as he might have treated a marble statue. As if she was some *thing* and not some *one.*

As she walked into the lofty lounge-hall Creena found her sister Norma arguing fiercely with their parents.

'I don't see why I must ride in the gymkhana if I don't want to . . .'

Creena paused in the doorway, looking round the comfortable, slightly shabby room with the thatched roof showing between the wooden beams, the chintz-covered chairs, the short golden curtains fluttering at the open windows. Her mother was in her rocking-chair, the knitting, that seldom left her busy fingers, lying on her lap for once, as she stared in dismay at her youngest child.

'But Norma, darling, you've always been so fond of riding . . .'

'Prince will feel out of things . . .' Creena's father said slowly, his fingers nervously fingering his red moustache, his eyes worried. 'It's so unlike you.'

Norma, short and dumpy in stained white jeans, backed away, standing with her back to the door. She stared at them both defiantly: 'Look—can't a person change?' she asked angrily. 'I'm . . . I'm growing up and if I think gymkhanas are rather childish . . .'

'Creena rides in them . . .' Mrs. Hall pointed out quietly.

'Oh, Creena . . .' Norma said bitterly. 'She can afford to . . . but I'm not going to and that's that . . .' She moved abruptly, swinging round, opening the door and going through it, slamming it behind her.

'Bill . . .' Mrs. Hall's voice was worried and then she saw Creena in the doorway. 'Darling,' she demanded, 'did you hear that extraordinary little scene?'

Creena nodded. She could understand her parents' bewilderment. All her life, Norma had been the tomboy of the family, adoring horses and dogs, hating pretty clothes and any social event. Suddenly, almost overnight, she had changed.

'What did she mean,' her mother demanded, 'when she said you could afford to ride? It costs her nothing . . . when I think

66

what we paid for Prince—and only last year your father bought her some very expensive riding boots and . . .'

Creena went to sit on the couch, smiling at her father as he filled his pipe. 'I don't know. I suppose it's just a phase,' she said mildly. 'I can remember when I just went off swimming . . . I was . . . well, sort of scared.'

'But Norma couldn't be scared of riding,' Mrs. Hall said, her voice dismayed. 'Why she rides beautifully—better than either you or Mike . . .'

'I wouldn't say that, my dear . . .' the doctor said mildly. 'Mike has the most gentle hands . . .'

Mrs. Hall flushed. 'I know . . . and you ride very well . . . too, Creena, but . . .'

Creena hesitated. She had a shrewd idea that what was stopping Norma from wanting to ride in public was the puppy-fat she had suddenly developed. In just over a year, she had gone from a skinny little girl to a dumpy fat one. No wonder the poor kid hated to be stared at by crowds of people. But would it be wise to tell the old people that? Creena decided against it. Her mother would only scold Norma for being supersensitive and point out that most girls in their teens got fat—her father would say she must not diet and would probably start watching to make sure she didn't . . . She decided to change the subject.

67

'How I hate that Mrs. Isipin . . .' she said almost violently.

It worked. 'Don't we all,' her mother said fervently.

'I sometimes wonder how that poor man stands her,' Dr. Hall said slowly. 'It's something pathological.'

'That's what Bart says . . .' Creena said, turning to him eagerly. 'You doctors are all the same—always looking for the reason behind people's behaviour. You won't just let them he nasty or moody or aggressive—you have to find out why.'

Her father began to laugh. 'That's our job,' and went on laughing so that it gave Creena a chance to slip away, dumping the basket of vegetables and fruit on the kitchen table, looking through the window and watching Violet, the African maid, chatting with the two garden boys as they filled their pails with poultry food and grain before going down to the poultry runs.

Back in her own room, Creena leant close to the mirror and studied her face anxiously. She was not vain at all but she knew that she was not ugly, yet now as she looked at the slanting green eyes that stared back at her, she wondered if she lacked that certain something. Never once had Bart treated her as anything but a *thing*—not at the hospital nor today. It was infuriating to be treated so impersonally. As if she just didn't exist—wasn't there. Was that how he behaved to all girls? Was that his defence against them? Was that why he was still single—why he had never fallen in love? Because he refused to see a girl as a girl . . . Oh, the man was infuriating . . .

CHAPTER FIVE

Creena was galloping along the race course with Mike, the wind stinging her cheeks, her hair flying behind her. Snow-White was in great form, she thought exultantly. She was looking forward to the gymkhana and wondered if this year, Dennis would ride. He had ridden in it the first two years he was there but last year, he had found an excuse not to do so. As usual, rumour was rife through the small town and there had been many reasons given for his defaulting. As he played polo every Sunday that he could, it was quite obvious that he was a very good rider. Unhappily Creena remembered her brother, Mike's opinion.

'Trouble with Dennis is,' he had said bluntly, 'he is a bad loser.' Then he had flushed uneasily and looked apologetically at his sister. 'I'm sorry, Creena.'

'You needn't be,' she had told him airily. 'Dennis is just a friend and you could be right.'

But it had worried her at the time and today

she remembered it vividly. Dennis loved doing anything at all so long as he was the tops—the bestest, as Norma would have put it. But he had come up against some very strong talent and had failed signally in events like sword-pegging and slicing the orange. This year he would have a good excuse—his bad arm. She wondered if Bart rode.

Mike slowed up as they approached the poles. 'Going to put 'em through it again?' he shouted, his short fair hair gleaming in the sunshine.

Creena nodded and laughed. 'Come on, girl . . .' she cried to her horse and she felt the strong muscles of the animal under her answer to her cry.

It was a heavenly day. Blue cloudless sky—sunshine—the background of green trees and the mountains as they climbed towards the sky.

An hour later they rode home slowly, talking as they walked.

'Creena'—seventeen-year-old Mike was suddenly shy—'is it true that you and Dennis are—'

Creena's green eyes were amused as she looked at him. 'Are what?'

He fidgeted in the saddle. 'Ah—go on, you know what I mean. Everyone in town are saying that you're going to marry that drip . . . eh . . . sorry, old girl.'

Creena half-closed her eyes for a moment. 'Okay, old boy,' she said lightly, and then she looked at him. 'Mike Hall,' she said gravely. 'You can tell the busy-bodies in the town that I am not going to marry Dennis Tyson.'

He heaved a sigh of relief. 'Thank God for that.'

Creena stared at him. 'You don't like him.'

'I most certainly do not,' Mike said violently. 'He's for the girls—why, even Norma drools when he looks at her.'

Creena's heart seemed to jerk. Could Norma be . . . or rather, could she think she was in love with Dennis? Oh, no! But girls these days seemed to grow up overnight. Look at how precocious Ailsa had been and she was barely seventeen. Norma was going on for fifteen. Was that the reason for this sudden interest in clothes and cosmetics, the shyness and self-consciousness about her changing figure, her plump hips? Oh, no . . . no . . . no! Yet, knowing Dennis, she was well aware that he would think it rather a joke to inspire a teen-age adoration, he might even encourage the child.

'Mike,' Creena said as they turned the horses to climb the last steep path to the paddock. 'I wish people wouldn't always couple my name with Dennis. He hasn't asked me to marry him and I'm not even sure that he wants to . . .'

'They say he does . . .' Mike said jerking his head towards the town that lay in the valley below. 'How come he's never said anything?'

71

'Well—we just sort of drifted along,' Creena said. 'I'm not even sure that he's ever thought of marriage. Dennis, you know, is an ambitious man. A wife might be a handicap.'

'Not the right sort of wife,' Mike said, slowing up King, bending down to unlatch the gate.

Prince, a young horse, was grazing placidly. Now he looked up at them.

'I hear Norma's not going to ride,' Mike said as he swung himself off the horse.

'M'm . . .' Creena murmured. 'It's her business.'

'Sure . . . sure . . . girls are queer critturs . . .' Mike commented and grinned at her. 'I'll see to things if you want to get on indoors.'

So it was that Creena walked down the steep gardenside and into the house alone, her cheeks flushed, her hair a tangle of curls, her slim body elegant in the well-cut jodhpurs, the shining boots, the white silk shirt. She paused in the doorway—the blue sky and green mountains framing her perfectly with her red-gold hair and fair skin.

'Oh . . . it's you . . .' she said lamely.

Bart Darling rose hastily from the couch where he had been sitting, reading the paper. He looked dazed, as if he had been half-asleep.

'Your father asked me to tea and—'

Creena began to laugh. 'Must have forgotten all about it. I am sorry . . .' she said,

72

entering the cool room. 'Mother has gone to a church meeting, I do know that. Look, do sit down and I'll get some tea for us in a moment. Mike is seeing to the horses and then he'll be down . . .'

'You're sure I'm not a nuisance . . .' the big, broad-shouldered man said slowly in a deep concerned voice. 'I expect your father has been caught up in some—'

'Game of golf,' Creena laughed. 'He has no sense of time . . .'

She went out to the large kitchen where the white table gleamed from fresh scrubbing and the big Esse stove filled one wall. Out of the back door and there was Violet, sitting on the grass in the sun, doing some of her interminable intricate and very beautiful crochet.

'Tea—Violet,' Creena called. 'For three or four.'

Violet was on her feet, coming down quickly, her dark face beaming. Violet loved company—it acted as a challenge.

So it was no surprise to Creena when, fifteen minutes later, Violet brought in a sumptuous tea—small flap-jacks, warm with jam and cream on them, cucumber sandwiches, three kinds of cake.

'Quite a feast,' Bart commented with a smile.

Mike chose that moment to come in and had to be introduced.

73

'Though I've seen you in town,' Mike said, his eyes frankly curious. 'Everyone's talking about you.'

Bart did not seem perturbed. 'I was brought up in a small town in England,' he told them. 'So I know what local curiosity is like.' He smiled. 'I'm sure some strange tales are going round.'

'Sure—sure . . .' Mike said, gulping down several flapjacks and then looked at his watch. 'Man!' He jumped to his feet. 'I'd better start my prep. Dad's on the warpath again . . .' He grinned at Bart. 'You any good at Latin?'

Bart was smiling. 'Pretty fair . . .' He looked sceptically at Mike: 'Don't tell me you have problems.'

'And how. Latin is such a dead language, gives me the creeps.'

'You need it—for so many things. Medicine, science . . .'

'I won't need it. I'm going to farm . . .'

Amidst laughter Mike retreated and left them alone. There was a little strained silence and then they both spoke at once—both stopped—then began again.

Creena had to laugh and suddenly Bart was laughing, too.

'Your turn,' she said, and re-filled his cup.

'I was going to say what a nice house this is—so comfortable and lived-in.' Ban looked round the whitewashed walls, at the oil paintings of past members of the family, of trees, sunsets. 'Very colourful.'

'Ma thinks it is very shabby but we haven't too much money,' Creena explained carefully. 'You see, Dad wants Mike to go to university and then there's Norma to educate.'

'Your father has retired?' Bart asked quietly.

Creena nodded. 'He had no choice. He had a thrombosis in his left eye and for a long time was practically blind. He went to Johannesburg and had an op. and it is better now but by no means perfect. He acts as locum at the hospital and assists at ops. but . . . but actually, he was advised to take things quietly.'

'He must have found it very hard.'

'He did.'

After they had finished tea, they went to sit on the stoep, talking easily. Creena was interested in what he told her—in the glimpse of his life that he gave her. It all began because Norma came into the room, took one glance at Bart and escaped. Bart looked a bit startled so Creena had to explain.

'Norma is going through a sensitive stage,' she said. 'I think the fact that she has put on so much weight and keeps getting spots is the cause. Ma is quite worried but I daren't tell her the reason because she fusses so. She'd keep on at Norma about not being silly and . . .'

She realized that Bart was annoyed about something for his voice was cold. 'Most mothers fuss—some more than others. It's usually because they want to help their children.'

Creena's cheeks were hot. 'I wasn't suggesting my mother fusses about nothing,' she said angrily. 'It's just that sometimes she fusses in the wrong way. Norma needs to be left alone. My mother is wonderful—she is not in the least possessive and—'

'I'm sure she is wonderful,' Bart said quietly. 'I have only to talk to your father to realize that. Not many doctors are lucky enough to have such an understanding wife. My father was a doctor and I don't think my mother ever forgave him for it.'

'Rosalie Pipp is like that,' Creena said. 'Have you met her?'

The faintest smile touched Bart's firm mouth. 'Very slight and very blonde and helpless?' he asked. 'Yes, I have met her.'

'Two years ago, Dr. Pipp gave us all the surprise of our lives when he married Rosalie,' Creena went on. 'We never thought she'd stick it out—it's pretty quiet here and he is old enough to be her father. We all wondered why she married him.'

'Perhaps she loved him,' Bart said quietly.

Again her cheeks burned. He had the most uncomfortable knack of putting her in the wrong. 'Well, maybe she did but she has a funny way of showing it. She's always quarrelling with him.'

'I think she resents his interest in his work.

He is a good doctor.'

Creena laughed. 'Dennis doesn't think so. He said his arm was badly set.'

A strange look flitted over Bart's face. 'I think he is mistaken,' he said quietly. And deliberately changed the subject. 'My mother hated the idea of my being a doctor—she did her best to stop me.' He smiled suddenly. 'I'm afraid I was too stubborn. I worked my way through medical school and she never forgave me.'

'How long have you been in Africa?'

'Seven years. I came out alone but later, my mother followed me.'

Quido, the big black Labrador, had wandered through the open outside-door of Mike's room and came to sit by Bart's side, his head on his knee, looking up at the big man with liquid brown eyes. Bart's hand found the right spot behind Quido's ear and his fingers moved gently as he went on talking.

'I used to get very angry with my mother,' he confessed slowly in his deep deliberate way. 'I thought she was a spoil-sport, was trying to ruin my life but one of the advantages of growing older is that you see things in the right perspective.' He paused—looking thoughtfully at the green mountains before him. Quido nudged him gently and obediently Bart began to scratch the dog's neck again. 'Sometimes,' he added, 'I must admit that I still lose my sense of proportion. Mother was a very lovely girl—unfortunately she was both jealous and possessive. She was a probationer at Guy's Hospital in London when she met my father.' He gave a deep chuckle. 'It must have gone to her head. The famous surgeon, an honorary consultant, asking her for the first dance at the hospital ball. My father was a very handsome man with a natural unconscious charm, he was wedded to his work but he fell in love with my mother, and then the trouble began.' He sighed, paused and devoted his attention to the dog.

Creena stared at the downbent head and saw with a sudden and unexpected tenderness that Bart's hair was so long that there were little soft curls on the nape of his neck. She must remind him to get his hair cut—yet it was a shame to chop off those curls. She had a sudden desire to touch them, to twist one round her finger. Shocked at the thought, she felt her cheeks flame and Bart chose that moment to look at her. He did not speak but simply stared and she felt her face get hotter and hotter. Could he read her thoughts? Guess the terrible thing she had wanted to do? When he spoke he startled her.

'Am I shocking you?' he asked in a gentle voice. 'You have been so very fortunate in having parents who are happily married.'

Her mouth was dry. It was difficult to speak. She had suddenly thought of something—and it was so absurd, so foolish, so . . . so out-of-this-world, that she was frightened. It could not be true. Things didn't happen so swiftly. It couldn't—mustn't be true . . .

'I know,' she said slowly. 'I've friends whose parents fight all the time. It is absolutely ghastly. Did your parents fight?'

He smiled. 'Far worse than that—they just didn't talk. I gather my mother was early disillusioned in her marriage. My father certainly loved her but he believed there was a time and a place for all things and that his work came first. Mother was very young and romantic and she believed he had stopped loving her—I gather there were tumultuous scenes and in the end they had me.' He laughed a little wryly. 'I suppose they thought that the pitter-patter of little feet might re-unite them. It rarely does. Mother let loose all her dammed-up love on me. I was the sun, moon and stars to her. As I grew up, she was fiercely protective. It was terrible. She hated me going to school—playing games, anything she called dangerous. Home was a nightmare to me. I couldn't get back to school quickly enough. They didn't fight but there would be a stony silence all through meals and my mother would complain to me of something my father had done. My youthful loyalty was terribly torn. As I grew older, my sympathies were with my father. You see, I had known from early days that I was going to be a doctor. My mother wanted me to be an accountant. The fights we had about that . . .'

'But . . . but as she was a nurse, she must have known that your father would have to devote himself to his work as a doctor,' Creena said tentatively.

Bart looked at her expressively. 'I think she could have accepted that had she been sure of my father's love for her. He was a man who found it hard to show emotion. He always seemed so . . . so impersonal . . .'

Creena caught her breath. It was funny but that was how Bart seemed to her. Impersonal.

'He died in a car crash,' Bart went on his voice devoid of emotion. 'It was like a slap in the face—the ground cut from under my feet. Somehow although we had never been very close. I had always known my father was there, that he would back me up. Of course my mother needed me more than ever. It was quite a problem.' His hand ran along the smooth silkiness of Quido's back. 'Your dogs are in excellent condition,' he said to Creena.

She caught her breath again. 'Please go on . . .' she said. 'How did you manage to become a doctor in the end?'

Bart smiled ruefully. 'My father had left me some money but I hadn't enough. I worked my way through medical school, working in the holidays, working all the time. I loved her . . . my mother, but I knew I had to become a doctor.'

A chill settled on Creena. She looked out at

the garden that was filled with flowers—great bushes of red hibiscus—beds of flowering stocks, blues, cream, yellow. The sun was still shining but she was cold.

'Go on,' she told him.

'Well—we had the most terrible fights and in the end she had a nervous breakdown.' He paused and smiled again. 'I'm afraid I didn't believe in the authenticity of that breakdown, my mother isn't a very good actress, anyhow it failed to achieve its purpose and when she saw that nothing would change me, she became a happy invalid and went to live with her sister.' He bent over the dog, opening the gentle mouth, looking at the animal's teeth, rumpling his head. 'You're a nice old boy . . .' he said softly, and then looked up. 'Well, I became a doctor—practised in England and then came out here. I was in East London when mother turned up, just as if we had never quarrelled. She said that she knew I needed her and so she had made an effort to recover her lost health and come out to me.'

'And did you need her?' Creena asked.

Bart's smile was so sweet that it was as if her heart jerked. 'Of course not. I need no one.' The words were said quietly. It was not a boast. Not a threat. Just a statement. But she knew it was the truth. She shivered. Bart did not need anyone. He was self-sufficient. She shivered again. Not that it mattered to her, of course, but . . .

He went on. 'Of course I played along with her. I had grown sufficiently mature to realize that she needed me, that her tyranny, her apparent selfishness was all part of her love for me. If only she had had a half-dozen children. If only all that pent-up love could have been divided. She never liked East London, or South Africa, but as she never failed to remind me, she stayed with me because I needed her. She still could not understand why I was often late for meals—why at the last moment I couldn't attend a cocktail party with her . . . she always saw these acts on my part as a deliberate attempt to hurt her.' He sighed. His face clouded over. 'And then . . .'

They had not heard the car draw up and suddenly Creena's parents were there. Mrs. Hall distressed and apologetic. Dr. Hall shaking Bart's hand warmly, also apologetic. 'Can't think how I could have forgotten, son.'

'I am sorry,' Mrs. Hall said sincerely, her face flushed, her greying hair wispy. 'I do hope Creena has been looking after you. I thought she was out riding with Mike and when Bill picked me up and said he had just remembered you, I was afraid you might have found an empty house.'

'He did, Ma,' Creena said. 'When I came back I found him patiently waiting so I gave him tea . . .'

'I am sorry,' Mrs. Hall said again. 'I know how precious your few hours of freedom are.'

'Oh, please,' Bart said, looking embarrassed. 'I was very happy here. Just relaxing. You've got a beautiful home . . .'

'Well,' Mrs. Hall said. Creena stifled a sigh. Her mother was 'flapping' as usual. 'You will stay to dinner . . . please. Dr. Darling, I really insist . . .' she stared up at the big man towering over her and smiled. 'Please. You can tell the hospital you are here.'

He smiled back. 'I already have. Thank you very much,' he said. 'I would like to . . .'

It was later that evening when they got back onto the subject of doctors and marriage again. Dinner had been a very pleasant meal— roast chicken, Creena had stifled a sigh and exchanged significant smiles with Mike and Norma for all of them were deadly tired of chicken, their mother's favourite standby for an unexpected guest. Strawberries from the garden, ice-cream. Norma had been very quiet and almost withdrawn, hardly talking once, eyeing Bart with a strange look of hostility. Mike had been full of talk, all about the coming gymkhana and their plans. Bart had admitted he could ride; 'Just . . .' he added with a smile. Then Mike and Norma had vanished and the others had sat in the large lounge hall, with the door open to the warm night, watching the great golden moon climb slowly in the sky above the dark mountains.

'I'm afraid I must have bored your daughter this afternoon,' Bart said with an apologetic

83

smile at Creena. 'I can't think why I went on like that—I don't usually talk so much,' he told her, half-laughing.

She smiled back at him, wondering if he noticed that the green of her simple silk frock exactly matched her eyes, if he saw her hair shining from the vigorous brushing she had given it, if he saw her at all. She very much doubted it.

'I found it most interesting . . .' she said truthfully and might have added, with equal truth, 'and extremely disheartening.' Which was absurd but . . .

'What were you talking about?' Bill Hall asked, slowly packing his pipe and asking a silent question of his wife, who sometimes said she loathed the smell of all pipes, just according to the mood she was in. But tonight she merely smiled back so he knew that she was relaxed, unworried, for once, about her children.

Bart laughed. 'Marriage,' he said.

Mrs. Hall's hands were clasped and they tightened as she looked at him.

'Marriage?' she asked, her voice sharp.

He nodded. 'I was just saying that a dedicated doctor should stay single. Not all men are as lucky as your husband, Mrs. Hall.'

Creena saw her mother flush—saw in her eyes a struggle between pleasure at the unexpected compliment and dismay at such a remark.

'I can't say I agree, Dr. Darling,' Mrs. Hall said. Her voice was a little sharp. 'It depends on the woman. The right woman can help a doctor.'

'And the wrong one can ruin him,' Bart said, his voice grim.

Creena sat quietly, Rudi on the couch by her side. He was twitching, his tail wagging excitedly. Probably in his dream he was chasing a rabbit—or a lovely sleek, silk-coated dasch like himself, except that it was a glamorous female for Rudi adored females and was always being torn to bits by other dogs and still bravely and foolishly going back into the fray. Lucky Rudi—he had his dreams.

It was a pleasant evening. Creena was in the kitchen getting coffee when the telephone bell rang. She had been listening to the conversation through the open door. Bart and her father were discovering that they shared a dream—a dream of starting a hospital that would be entirely run by Africans. African doctors, surgeons, anaesthetists, pathologists, nurses. Listening she had thought how very different Bart was from Dennis. Dennis who loathed the African side of the hospital and left it to the other doctors when he could.

As she heard his deep voice talking on the telephone, Creena knew it was a call for Bart. She lifted the steaming saucepan of coffee off the stove and went through to the lounge.

'Have you time to drink your coffee?' she

asked.

Bart was saying good-bye to her mother, receiving an invitation to drop in when he liked. Now he smiled at the pretty girl in the doorway.

'I'm afraid not,' he said.

'Show Bart down to the car with the torch, Creena,' Dr. Hall said, tapping out the warm ashes in his pipe. 'The torch is on the stoep shelf—those stairs are tricky until you know 'em . . .'

It was a warm night—the gorgeous moon turning the landscape into fairy magic—the great trees stark against the sky. The frogs were beginning to croak—that was supposed to mean rain.

Creena led the way down the stone steps, shining the torch light. At Bart's car she waited while he got in. She could see his face in the moonlight but it looked different, softer, more . . . more human.

'Thanks for a very enjoyable day, Creena,' he said quietly.

The colour stung her cheeks. 'I . . . I . . . enjoyed it, too,' she said lamely and wished she could think of something brilliant to say. Something that would make him see her as a person.

'It's wonderful to be in a home, to relax, to feel no tensions, no undercurrents of suppressed emotion,' he went on slowly. 'You are a very lucky girl, Creena, to have such parents.'

'Yes, I know I am . . .' she said.

All this lovely moonlight and all he could say was that she had wonderful parents. She thought of how Dennis would behave with any pretty . . . pretty girl. She caught her breath. But wasn't that just it? *Any* pretty girl?

'When are you coming back to work, Creena?' Bart asked abruptly.

The question was so far removed from her thoughts that it was like a jolt. Had his voice a note of criticism?

'I . . .' She might have pointed out that he had told her to take things quietly—that her father had said after such a shock, she should go easy. He gave her no time.

His voice was unexpectedly harsh. 'The work is piling up. Matron complains she is having to do your work as well as hers—there's quite a muddle.'

Creena stared at him and for a moment she hated him with all her heart. Always he twisted things so that she was in the wrong. Why? Why must he . . .

'I'll be back on Monday, Dr. Darling,' she said coldly and turned away.

As she climbed the steep stone stairway, she thought she heard him call her name, but it was so unlikely that she dismissed it as impossible, and went on, seething inwardly with humiliation and anger. Had he seen the thoughts on her face? Had he noticed the way she looked at the beautiful moon? Had he spoken like that deliberately to remind her that he was a doctor—dedicated and opposed to marriage? That he disliked women and their romantic notions, that . . .

She hurried through the lounge, not wanting her parents to see her disturbed face. 'I'll pour the coffee,' she said over her shoulder, and busied herself in the kitchen until she felt more composed again.

CHAPTER SIX

On Monday morning Creena was punctually at her desk in the small room off the entrance hall to the hospital. It was not a very nice day—the blue sky marred by piling cumulus clouds that promised a storm. She sat behind her desk in her white coat and studied the appalling mass of work that had accumulated in the few weeks of her absence. Had Matron attempted to tackle anything at all? It didn't look like it . . .

With a sigh, Creena dived into the work, opening and sorting the mail, her mind engrossed, her face absorbed as she bent over the papers.

'Nice to have you back,' Meg Gordon said suddenly.

Creena looked up with a start. Sister Meg

Gordon was in the doorway, smiling at her, tall, a little stately, with black hair smoothed back and twisted into a neat bun. On Meg's serene face there was never any trace of the difficulties she had to face with a full-time job and an invalid demanding mother at home.

'Good film on Saturday, wasn't it,' Meg said chattily.

'Very good,' Creena said but for some strange and ridiculous reason, she found herself colouring as she gazed into Meg's eyes.

On Saturday, as usual, the entire Hall family had piled into the big shabby car and driven down into Klomati, the little nearby dorp. Bioscope was always held in the old Court House and as usual, many people took folding chairs in the backs of their cars for the size of the building was far too small to comfortably hold all the inhabitants of the little town. Again as usual the Halls had their usual seats—next door to Audrey Hamilton and her father and as Mrs. Isipin had put it, 'temporary' stepmother, and just behind where Dennis usually sat. When the lights went out, the croaking of the frogs and the buzz of flying insects had vied with the sound track but no one seemed to mind. In the dark, two people had gone into the seats in front of Creena and it wasn't until the lights went up that Creena saw that it was Bart and Meg. The second-half of the film need never have been shown so far as it affected Creena for she saw little of it.

She was gazing at the back of Bart's head—she had to lean sideways to see round him and kept getting tantalizing glimpses of his profile when he leaned down to speak to Meg. Now why had he taken Meg . . . yet he had every right to do so. And Creena was glad, very glad, that Meg was having a night out for a change. It was so seldom she could leave her mother. Yet if Bart was determined to remain a bachelor—was it a very good idea? She had twisted and almost torn a hankie in her restless hands as she sat there and she had had quite a job convincing her other foolish self that to take Meg to the bioscope meant nothing, nothing at all. And if it did, it was no business of hers—none at all.

Now Creena could not resist saying: 'It was good, wasn't it. Nice to see that you are managing to get out occasionally.'

Meg smiled serenely. 'That was Dr. Darling's doing. He came to see Mother and asked me if I was going to the film and when I explained why I could not, he arranged for one of those Portuguese women from the Mill to come and sit with her. I do think it was good of him. He even drove Mrs. Cortez home afterwards.'

'Very good of him,' Creena said and managed a gay smile. 'He's nice, isn't he?' she asked lightly.

A faint flush swept Meg's pale cheeks. 'That,' she said slowly and then turned away, 'is the understatement of the season.'

Creena watched Meg walking down the corridor. How gracefully she moved, how well her uniform suited her. She was a beautiful woman . . . perhaps Bart thought so. It had certainly been very thoughtful of him . . .

She turned back to the papers again. If only she could stop thinking about him. Meg would make a wonderful doctor's wife . . .

'Good morning, Miss Hall.' A deep voice made her jump. As she looked up, she found Bart standing in the doorway staring at her. 'Afraid it's somewhat of a mess, isn't it?' His voice was quite sympathetic as he stared at the pile of papers.

Creena managed a smile. She always had the strange feeling that he could read her thoughts—and if he could . . . She swallowed. 'I don't know what Matron did—'

'Precious little, I'm afraid,' Bart said almost curtly. There—how easily it happened. He seemed to be always picking on her—now he was implying that she was moaning because Matron hadn't done enough! 'I'm afraid . . .' he went on, lowering his voice discreetly, 'that our Matron is inclined to flap. Now I wonder if you could hunt out the notes about several patients I have to see today?' He gave her a piece of paper on which were neatly printed a few names. He looked at his watch. 'I'm going over to the African out-patients now. If you could send them over, sometime.'

'Of course, Dr. Darling,' Creena said quickly. She sat very still as she watched him walk down the corridor. How slowly he seemed to move—yet how rapidly he covered the ground. His big broad-shouldered figure seemed to fill the narrow corridor.

She was kept busy for the next hour, answering the telephone, booking appointments, making out receipts. It only took her a few moments to find the case histories Bart had asked for and—on a sudden impulse, she decided against sending one of the African orderlies, immaculate in their starched white coats and trousers, with it, but carried it herself to the African out-patients.

It was not a big hospital but it was built in the shape of an L, the small part being the European section, the longer part the African. This was always full—and as she walked rapidly down the corridor past the wards, she glanced through the glass walls at the conglomeration of patients. In the women's wards, most of the women had had babies and there was a wailing mixed up with a chattering; in the men's wards, there were ambulatory patients meandering around, wearing long white night-shirts, many with small knitted woollen caps perched on their heads. The flashing of white teeth in dark brown faces— the rolling of the whites of eyes in the dark faces of the children—the colourful blankets some of the patients had draped round them, all made a picture that was hard to forget.

The short enormously-fat African orderly in charge of out-patients, admitted Creena into the small surgery. Bart looked up. He had a small black child on the couch and was bending over him. He looked up.

'Thanks—you shouldn't have brought it yourself.'

Creena smiled at him. 'What's wrong with the child?' she asked.

'Come and look . . .' Bart invited.

By his side, she stared down at the child. He was probably about three—a plump, well-fed child with shining eyes and a friendly smile. Bart's hand slid gently down the little legs and Creena caught her breath with dismay as her eyes followed the movement of Bart's fingers.

The little African boy had club feet. Not one but both feet were pitifully deformed. His mother stood to one side, she wore a drooping red skirt and a torn white blouse. She was twisting her hands and speaking to Benjamin, the orderly. Creena's knowledge of Swazi was rather limited but she gathered a certain amount of what the mother was saying and a cold finger ran down her spine. The boy's father blamed her for the child's feet—he had threatened to have the child killed . . . she was afraid.

'I don't suppose anything can be done, can it?' Creena asked softly, letting the little boy cling to her finger and then let go of it again.

She spoke to the boy in Swazi, asking him his name. She turned away for a moment. Poor little Elias.

'I think it can be done . . .' Bart said—in a voice she had never heard him use before. It was an authoritative voice—a voice that seemed to be challenging someone or something. 'I'm going to put both legs in plaster casts. There is a new technique—'

Meg was suddenly at his elbow. 'Dr. Tyson has seen the case, Dr. Darling,' she said softly. 'He said it was inoperable.'

'It may be inoperable . . .' Bart said almost curtly. 'But that doesn't eliminate—'

'Dr. Tyson seemed to think it would be a waste of time . . .' Meg said, her voice silkily soft.

Creena looked at her quickly. Meg's eyes were fixed on Bart's face, her expression strange. Why must she keep harping on what Dennis had said? Why repeat it in that tone.

'I still think we have a good chance,' Bart said, his voice even more curt and crisp. 'Now the first thing is to make his mother understand the importance of . . .'

Creena left the case histories on the table, signalling to the Orderly-in-Charge, that they were there and quietly left the room. Bart had already forgotten she existed.

Back at her desk, she listened to the distant rumble of thunder and tried to forget the disquiet she had felt in the surgery. But why had Meg spoken like that . . . why . . .

In the days that followed, she constantly saw Bart and yet never seemed to see him at all. A fleeting figure hurrying with his deceptive casualness past her room—a flick of his fingers—a curt: 'Good morning, Miss Hall,' and that was all. Yet at the same time she could not get away from him. Everywhere she went—in the hospital or in the small town, someone would talk about the new doctor. Of course, as her father dryly said, new brooms are exciting but the number of appointments Creena had to make for Bart's few precious private surgery hours was amazing. It was as if everyone with an old complaint was hoping that the new doctor would produce some new or magic medicine to cure their ills. When she had got her work up-to-date, Creena often wandered down to the European wards and chatted with the patients. They were all people she had known for many years. The wards were small—each with two beds, but they were light airy cheerful little rooms; there was a wide veranda, too, for sitting-up patients to be wheeled to or for walking patients to bask in the sun. Everywhere it was the same story. The new doctor.

'A fine man . . .'

'Doesn't pull his punches. I like a man who's not afraid to tell you the truth.'

'He makes one feel safe—he is a doctor you can trust.'

'He's terribly smooth, isn't he. My blood pressure goes up the instant he comes into the room. I only hope he doesn't guess why...'

'I wish he was more friendly—he's always so ... sort of distant...'

Everyone had something different to say about him. It was almost comical how often some of the remarks clashed. Where Bart would impress one man, he would anger another by his frank insistence on adherence to a strict diet; where one woman would say how kind he was, another woman would shrug and say that he had a very strange bed-side manner. Mrs. Isipin, in again with more trouble to do with her sprained ankle, was the only one who said really nasty things. She cornered Creena one day, limping with much display of pain down the corridor to Creena's office, making some excuse about a mistake in her account, leaning heavily on the desk so that Creena was forced to ask her to sit down.

'There must be a mistake, Creena,' Mrs. Isipin snapped as she lowered herself carefully into the chair.

There was a sudden flurry outside the little office and there was Bart hurrying by, his face grim, his white cap tipped back on his thick fair hair, a gauze mask dangling beneath his chin. The shapeless tight-waisted white gown was stained. He looked in at the two women but it was obvious that he did not see them. His mouth was a thin line, his eyebrows drawn

96

together in fury.

'In a hurry,' Mrs. Isipin said with a sniff. 'Where are his manners.'

'It's an emergency operation,' Creena explained. 'They've just wheeled the patient back to the ward . . .'

'He's a strange man,' Mrs. Isipin said, her voice thoughtful. She shot a quick glance towards Creena. 'What does your father think of him?'

Creena could feel the blood rushing to her cheeks. She clenched her hands. She must not lose her temper. She must not . . .

'My father admires Dr. Darling very much,' she said stiffly.

'So do a great many people. I find him very pleasant, very understanding but . . .' Mrs. Isipin paused, her eyes very bright with curiosity. 'Where did Dennis meet him in the first place? What does Dennis know about him?'

Creena had to dig her nails into her hands. 'I really don't know.'

'It's just that it seems rather odd that a doctor can down tools and everything and rush up here at twenty-four hours notice,' Mrs. Isipin went on slowly. 'I understand Dennis sent him a wire and he came the next day. If he had his own practice how could he arrange that . . .'

Creena ran her tongue nervously over her lips. Her temper was rising.

'The usual practice is to get a locum,' she said still more stiffly.

Mrs. Isipin stared at her. 'I know that, of course. But why . . . I mean, we all know how mean Mrs. Crampton is—he'd be getting a mere pittance . . .'

Creena swallowed again. 'Why don't you ask him, Mrs. Isipin,' she said quietly. 'I'm afraid I'm not in Dr. Darling's confidence.'

'Perhaps Meg is . . .' Mrs. Isipin leaned forward, her voice quiet. 'He goes there a great deal.'

'Her mother is sick . . .' Creena said wearily.

Mrs. Isipin stared at her. 'Of course I know she is sick—has been for years. Dennis realized long ago that she was a chronic case and it is waste of time trying to help her . . .'

'Perhaps Bart . . . I mean, Dr. Darling thinks differently. Every doctor has a different approach to each patient, so my father says,' Creena said.

It was a joyous relief when the telephone bell shrilled and she had to hurry and find Dr. Pipp. 'I'll check up on your account,' she promised Mrs. Isipin and escaped gladly. She found she was trembling with anger. That hateful beastly woman—why must she always be so suspicious, have such a nasty tongue. Did she enjoy upsetting people? Digging in little poisonous darts that would lie there and later fester.

It was the same in the town. Every time she

went into a shop, one of the assistants would mention the new doctor. At the hotel, the receptionist raved about him. A very young, pertly pretty girl, she told Creena confidentially that she thought the new doctor was awfully smooth and that it was most frightfully exciting to have him living there at the hotel and wasn't it bad luck the way they got him out of bed, nights, to go to the hospital or someone sick, how could he do his work when he never got enough sleep? At the many cocktail parties held in the town and neighbourhood to which Creena and her mother usually went, they would often meet Bart—he would seem to drift in, be there for a while and then drift out quietly again. On the golf course, he would often play a few holes with Dr. Hall and then say he had to go and stalk off back to his car. It was as if he wanted to be part of the local life and yet not get involved. He was friendly with everyone but friends with no one. He often visited Creena's home but rarely when she was there—he usually went up when he had a spare hour and would sit in the garden with Dr. Hall, talking *shop.*

It was strange, Creena thought, but to the quiet little town, Bart had come like a small explosion—making an impression on everyone for a short while and then quietly drifting to become part of the background. As the weeks passed and Bart was accepted by the local people, so that talk about him seemed to cease and yet, although his name was no longer on everyone's lips, yet she knew that everyone was vividly aware of him and of the difference his coming to the district had made. It was common property—the news that almost daily he and Mrs. Crampton fought. Most of the local people approved and were glad that there was someone to stand up to the tyrannical old woman. A few disapproved, saying that the way of diplomacy always obtained better results. The hospital had been stirred—anger, defiance and then obedience sweeping through it like a cold breeze but Bart had his way in the end. New and important sanitary arrangements had been made—a totally new outlook towards asepsis, a tighter ring of discipline, a more forceful approach to patients who disobeyed orders.

Janice Hames once dropped by Creena's office looking grim.

'That man has just pulled three strips off me and in front of the patient, too,' she said angrily, her white hair ruffled, her lovely face disturbed. 'I know I did wrong—I forgot something important but'—she bit her lip—'You should have seen his face, his eyes—heard the way he spoke. As if I was a . . . a dog.' She turned away. 'When . . . when is Dennis coming back, Creena? I'll be so thankful—he'll soon put that that man in his place.'

Creena sat silently, amazed at Janice's anger.

'Don't you know when Dennis is coming back?' Janice insisted, her eyes flashing. 'Doesn't he write to you?'

'I've heard three times,' Creena admitted. 'But he gives no date. His arm is healing well, now, but there can be no question of surgery or using it for some time, apparently. He is rather fed-up.'

'I'm sure he is. Poor Dennis.' Janice's voice softened. She turned away. 'Give him my love when you write,' she said casually over her shoulder as she hurried down the corridor.

Janice gone, Creena was free to think. Was Janice right? Would Dennis refuse to let Bart go on as he was doing—as if he was in charge of the hospital? Which he was, in point of fact. Although he was a locum, he was the only resident full-time doctor on the premises. It would be out of the question to put Dr. Pipp in charge—for he was only there so many days a week, having more or less retired from public practice, but still keeping a few private patients for himself. So Bart was in charge, and he had the right to make any necessary alterations for the patients' good or for the well-being of the hospital—but what would happen when Dennis returned? Would the two work in harmony? Or would Bart return to East London . . .

She put the cover over her typewriter and

101

wondered why she suddenly felt desolate. She could not say it was because she would miss Bart for she rarely saw him now and never alone. But this stupid vague feeling persisted . . . this strange happiness she felt just to be under the same roof as Bart.

She drove home slowly—through the little town with its dusty roads and the crowded colourful market, past the groups of African school children walking home, past the trees that were a mass of blue flowers, past the small river, towards her home. She climbed the stone steps slowly.

Her mother hurried to meet her, her face alight with excitement.

'Dennis is 'phoning you tonight, Creena,' she said eagerly. 'He's booked a personal call for eight o'clock. Perhaps he's coming back soon. Won't you be glad? You've had such a dull life lately . . .'

The dogs had raced to meet her—great Samson leaning heavily against her leg, slobbering lovingly at her hand, Rudi leaping up and down like a jack-in-the-box, Quido, more sober, lying down, looking up at her.

Was she glad? Was she even half as excited as her mother at the thought that Dennis might be coming back? Had she missed him? Had she had a dull life lately?

As in a dream, Creena answered vaguely and went to her room, there to sit heavily down on the bed and stare into space. Dennis might be coming back—he was most certainly coming back at some time in the near future. How was she going to feel? To behave?

She jumped to her feet impatiently. Why must she always cross her bridges long before the foundation stones were laid? Dennis might have forgotten the whole thing—forgotten her. Why worry about what might happen ...

But that night when she heard Dennis's warm eager voice in her ear, she knew that not only were the foundation stones of her bridge laid but that someone must have performed the opening ceremony for now the bridge would have to be crossed.

'I'll be home the day after tomorrow, darling,' Dennis said. 'I can't wait to see you again, darling,' he went on ardently. 'And ... and I've got a surprise for you! Don't they always say a girl's best friend is a diamond? Well, I've got a real whopper for you to wear on the third finger of your left hand. Be seeing you, darling, very soon.'

CHAPTER SEVEN

The next day was very hot and everything seemed to go wrong. After a bad night in which she had many dreams, Creena felt very weary and miserable. It did not help matters to have her mother be so very bright and almost coy at breakfast, every now and then commenting on Dennis's return and then looking worried as if she might have said too much.

Driving reluctantly to the hospital for she had to work Saturday mornings, Creena thought of the warmth in Dennis's voice on the telephone. Was he really serious? Did he believe she loved him? Did he want to marry her? Why had she this feeling of doubt, this absurd feeling that Dennis was playing a part? He might have been, at the hospital—but to whom would he have to play a part in Johannesburg.

Settling herself at her desk, she looked out at the close-cut lawns round the hospital and at the little band of African convicts who were tidying up the grounds in their striped shirts and shorts. They were laughing and talking happily and exchanging jokes with the walking patients in their white nightshirts. As usual there was a long queue of African women in their bright clothes, mostly with piccanins on their backs or small children clinging to their skirts. Creena frowned as she noticed one familiar face—a fat old African woman who had once worked as wash-girl for her mother, by her hand she had a small six-year-old girl who was jumping up and down. Creena realized vaguely that she had often seen the child at the out-patients and wondered who was sick, the granny or the child.

'You must be thrilled . . .' a voice said and Creena swung round. Janice was standing there, her uniform crisp and her eyes strange.

'Thrilled?'

Janice nodded. 'Because Dennis is coming back.'

'Oh!' Creena was aware that she had coloured. She hadn't been thinking of Dennis—indeed she had deliberately stopped thinking about him. It was all too absurd, she had decided during the long night, there was no need to have this feeling of panic; no one could force her to marry Dennis if she didn't love him. 'Yes—how did you know?' she asked without thinking.

It was Janice's turn to colour. 'Because Mrs. Crampton went off to Jo'burg last Tuesday to bring the erring boy home. She said it was nonsense the treatment for his arm taking so long—it could easily be continued here. So I knew Dennis was on his way back because he always does what Mrs. Crampton says . . .' She laughed—an ugly sound, Creena thought uneasily. 'I also hear,' Janice went on, her mouth twisting, 'that Dennis 'phoned you last night.'

Creena's cheeks were hot with anger. 'This is a shocking place,' she exploded. 'One can't even have a telephone call without the town knowing about it.'

Janice smiled almost triumphantly. 'The worst of having Gwen Nettlefold on night duty at the telephone exchange. She's so bored, she just listens in.'

'All the same, it is disgraceful,' Creena said fiercely. 'I mean . . . one might have something you didn't want everyone to know . . .'

Janice laughed outright. 'Hopeless to try that in Klomati—no one can have a secret here.' She walked away with a slight swing to her slim hips. Creena had a feeling that Janice had somehow scored over her yet could not think in what way.

She began to type a letter furiously. Sometimes she hated Klomati and all the tittle-tattle that went on. It wasn't that you wanted secrets but you did need a little privacy.

A car drew up outside and Creena looked up. She recognized Emily Caron instantly, a slight pale blonde girl who suffered from asthma. She was being helped out of her car by her husband, a great burly man with thick black hair, his khaki shirt open in front showing the tangled black hair on his chest, his khaki shorts cut very short, revealing great massive hairy thighs.

'Emily's pretty sick, Creena,' he said gruffly. 'Can you cope? I've got to get some things on the bus and I haven't much time . . .'

Creena was out of her little office, her arm round the girl. 'Of course, Piet.'

He hesitated. 'She seems worse when I'm around,' he said awkwardly. 'And I must get

106

that bus.'

'Go ahead,' Creena told him cheerfully. Emily walked with great difficulty down the corridor to the surgery. It was obvious that she could hardly breath. It was with relief that Creena saw that Bart was there—he looked up and instantly took over.

In a moment, Emily was on the couch—and Bart was giving her an injection. Almost immediately Emily's breathing became easier and soon she was smiling at the tall broad-shouldered man who was so very gentle with her. 'So silly of me . . .' she said, her pale face colouring. 'It isn't even as if I was really—'

'Asthma can be pretty unpleasant,' Bart said, going to the basin to wash his hands.

Creena slipped hack to her desk and in a short while, Emily came down the corridor, Bart by her side. He walked with his usual deceptive slowness, bending down to talk to the girl. She was shaking her head and he took her arm. Creena, bent over a ledger, heard him say: 'But as your doctor I insist, Emily. I know it can be arranged. Piet will manage . . .'

He saw the girl out to his car and drove away. In ten minutes he was back again, brushing his hand through his thick fair hair, pausing to look down at Creena. 'What can you do with a case like that?' he asked her quietly. 'Whatever made her marry Piet? Or Piet marry her? They're just so incompatible it's not true.'

'I suppose they fell in love,' Creena said carefully.

He shrugged. 'I'm sure they did and then woke up. Piet really means to be kind to her but he's so huge and he shouts his head off, not meaning a word of what he says and she quivers like a bit of thistledown, believing he means it. You know why she has asthma every evening?' he asked quietly, bending down towards Creena, his eyes concerned. 'Why it suddenly came on an hour ago because Piet unexpectedly went home for something he had forgotten? It was because he was in a tearing hurry and yelled at her for letting him forget! Any sane woman would have yelled back and told him he was old enough to remember things for himself but poor little Emily sort of crumpled at the knees and felt guilty because as usual, she had failed him and then found she was having an attack . . . that made it worse, for Piet could ill spare the time to bring her here but he got frightened when she was so bad . . .' Bart ran his hand through his thick hair wearily. 'What can I do? Advise her to leave him? Advise him to tone down his voice? Knock their heads together in the hope of beating a little sense into them?'

Creena stared at him curiously. Inside her there was a strangely sweet breathlessness. It was so rarely that Bart bothered to stop and talk to her.

'Can fright and . . . and emotional feeling

108

give you asthma suddenly like that?'

He nodded. 'Of course. That's why it's so much better for a doctor to know his patient's family and background. Often it is someone near them, a mother-in-law, a difficult father, a jealous husband—often a secondary figure is the cause for your patient's illness and if you can put the background right . . .'

'Not so easy.'

He laughed. 'How right you are, Creena. I'm going to get Piet to send her down to the coast for a few months. He'll agree but she says a wife's place is with her husband . . .' He turned and walked away and then came back. An odd look on his face. 'Creena—what are you doing this afternoon? I thought of going out to *Jackie's* for a swim. Care to come along?'

Creena caught her breath. Under her desk she crossed her fingers. Could it be true? Was Bart asking her to go out with him?

'I'd love to . . .' she said breathlessly.

He gave her his slow sweet smile. 'Good— I'll pick you up at half-past two. I promised to teach Mike a new dive—he'll be there.'

Creena's heart sank with a bump. Oh, so then she was simply part of the family. 'Isn't Norma coming too?' she asked sarcastically.

Bart didn't seem to notice the change in her tone. He ran his hand through his hair. 'I didn't think of asking her. Maybe she'd like to—you could ask her at lunch, couldn't you?'

She watched him walk away, she was breathing fast. How dared he . . . and then, as suddenly as it had come, her anger vanished. Bart was just being his usual discreet, woman-wary self. Playing safe. Take the family along and maybe people will overlook the fact that you are out with an attractive young woman. Suddenly she was laughing—and although she laughed until the tears came to her eyes, somehow it didn't seem to be very funny.

Creena was waiting for Bart when he called for her that afternoon, her green swimsuit already on beneath the candy-striped pink and white shorts and white shirt. Norma had said she didn't want to go swimming, and particularly not with that man. For some strange reason, Norma seemed to dislike Bart, Creena wondered why.

Bart arrived on the dot of half-past two. He looked larger than ever in spotless white shirt and shorts. He smiled at her. 'I'm really looking forward to this . . .' he said as he helped her in the car.

She was still angry with him. 'Aren't you afraid someone will talk?'

He looked startled as he backed the car and then drove over the cattle trap. And then his face cleared. He laughed. 'I get it. I don't think I really care so long as you don't mind.' He looked down at her red-gold hair, so soft and gleaming, at her oval eager little face, her strangely slanting green eyes and wondered why she smiled at him in such an odd way. Almost—almost as if she hated him. 'I'm afraid in a small place like this one has only to talk to a member of the opposite sex to set all sort of rumours going round.' He drove well, she noticed. Not fast but not slow—just a comfortable speed. She looked at his long thin fingers on the steering wheel and she gave a little shiver. Such strong yet gentle fingers. He chuckled. 'Creena—do you remember the night I sat at the bioscope in front of you? Meg was by my side.'

'I remember . .' Creena told him. Would she ever forget? It was the swift pang of jealousy she had felt that had warned her of what was happening. That she was in great danger of falling in love with a man who did not believe in marriage.

He chuckled again. 'Everyone thought I took her. Actually I was quite surprised to find her next to me.'

Creena looked at him. Was he lying? If so, why?

'Meg told me you made it possible for her to go.'

'Quite right. It's absurd the way she makes a martyr of herself over her mother. Her mother does not want her to and it merely makes Meg bitter and everyone sorry for her.' He paused, glancing down at Creena's face. 'Am I shocking you? Do you see Meg as a sweet dutiful daughter, unselfishly giving up her happiness

111

for the sake of her mother? Look, Creena, Meg is a good woman, lovely to look at, warm and friendly, but she is a masochist—she deliberately forfeits her own pleasures for her mother and she gets a great deal of gratification out of the feeling of being a good daughter. Whereas in very truth, she is harming her mother in several ways. First, by making her dependent on her. Secondly, by giving everyone the impression that the old lady is a very selfish person. In fact, the reverse is true. Meg sometimes irritates her mother to the point of screaming and the old lady told me quite tearfully that she only wished she was well enough to live alone because sometimes she felt she couldn't go on. She said if only Meg would make some friends, would go out, would stop clinging to her. That was why I arranged for the Portuguese woman to baby-sit. It isn't necessary. Old Mrs. Gordon is not so ill that she cannot be left—it is just that Meg refuses to leave her alone.'

'But . . . but . . .' Creena hesitated. Bart was giving her a whole new conception of Meg and her mother. Now, thinking as Bart drove along the winding dusty road to *Jackie's.* Creena remembered something her father had said once. He had said that he was sure that two-thirds of Mrs. Cordon's invalidism was due to Meg's solicitude.

'If only the girl would leave her mother alone and stop fussing, Mrs. Gordon would have a chance to stand on her own two feet and everyone would be happier.'

He had also said, Creena remembered now, that love was a strange thing. So often the last thing it thought of was the other person's happiness.

'Meg Gordon is a case in point. She loves her mother dearly but she wants her to be happy in her way—not in her mother's way. Mrs. Gordon would like to go into an old ladies' home. She is very garrulous, loves to have people around her, to hear their life histories, likes playing games of cards. To Meg, that would be ultimate horror. Her mother put in an old ladies' home? What would everyone say? What sort of daughter would she be . . . And so they go on like this.'

At the time, Creena had thought little of what he said. To her, the thought of an old ladies' home was repugnant. Now she wondered. Mrs. Gordon must be very lonely, there in that cottage way outside the town all alone all day except for the housegirl.

'Love is a funny thing, isn't it,' Creena said abruptly.

Bart looked down at her. 'What makes you say that?'

'Oh, just thinking about Meg and her mother,' Creena said and then told him what her father had said.

Bart looked interested. 'He might have something there, you know. I am sure Mrs.

Gordon would be much happier away from Meg and with people of her own age. I wonder if I could talk Meg into—'

Creena could not resist a little laugh. 'You could talk Meg into anything,' she said curtly.

They were reaching *Jackie's* now. Driving down the narrow road running along the mountainside, turning to face the wide thatched-roof building by the side of the swimming pool. There were quite a few people there already, sprawled on the grass or sitting at the small tables round the pool, the striped red and white sunshades tilted to shade them from the fierceness of the sun.

'Meg?' Bart echoed, his voice puzzled and then he was parking the car, helping Creena out of it, leading the way to the water's edge and somehow the conversation seemed to die a natural death.

Jackie's was a combined motel and coffee-house, run by a married couple called Kennedy who had the knack of attracting people and making them their friends for life. Paul Kennedy was as lean and skinny as his wife was short and fat but they treated the whole concern with a deceptively careless manner that made them almost appear to be guests at the hotel rather than the manager and manageress. Now Paul was in a swim suit, diving in the pool—he lifted his hand in greeting as he saw Creena and Bart arrive. Bart found a spare sunshade and dug it in the ground, spreading a towel on the grass for Creena to lie on and side by side, they stretched out in the warm air, talking lightly, listening to the shouts and laughter from the pool.

Half an hour later, Mike showed up with several friends and reluctantly Bart stood up, and wandered off to the changing room, coming back in a moment in his swim briefs and diving into the water. Creena watched him, sitting up, hugging her knees, listening to the shouts as Mike and his friends tried to follow Bart's expert diving. Creena sighed. Maybe all doctors were the same. Bart was standing her up in just the same way as Dennis had done at the dance. Why did a man take a girl out and then jettison her? She sighed. Maybe it was the girl's fault—maybe she lacked that certain something that made a man stick to a girl, never leaving her side.

But she was wrong. Within ten minutes, Bart was back by her side, asking her to go and swim with him, and for the rest of the afternoon he hardly left her, including her in everything, getting Mike and his friends sprawling on the grass round them as they all talked casually, but never forgetting for one moment that he was escorting Creena. It gave her a warm pleasant glow. Bart was so natural—so easy to talk to—there was no feeling of tension, no fear lest she say the wrong thing. It was obvious that Mike and his

115

friends liked him and when they drifted away in search of ice-cold Cokes, she told Bart so.

'Mike isn't easy to get on with,' she said. 'He's like me, got a quick temper and is always getting involved in fights.'

Bart rolled over and rested his chin on his hands, looking at her thoughtfully. 'Do you get involved in fights easily?'

She nodded. 'Especially if I think someone is being unfairly treated.'

Bart looked rueful. 'So do I. I just shoot off my mouth and later wish I'd taken the more diplomatic way.'

Creena stretched out lazily. 'Can you analyse the difference between diplomacy and—'

'Bart—Bart.' Mike was by their side, his voice urgent. 'A friend of mine just called and said his dog has been bitten by a snake. He can't get hold of Adams, he's the Vet. you know. I wondered if you . . .'

Bart sat up. 'Of course.' He was on his feet and then he hesitated, looking down at Creena. 'I can't just leave you here—'

She was on her feet. 'I'll be two seconds— just get dressed. I'll come with you. You won't have time to come back for me . . .'

She was as good as her word. Bart was just revving the engine as she slipped into the front seat by Mike's side.

Bart's face was grim. 'How long ago did it happen—what kind of snake—good thing I've

116

got my bag along with me . . .' He grinned for a moment, and added, 'I always take it along—my little outings are always doomed to be broken up.'

'I say, I am sorry . . .' Mike began.

Bart grinned. 'Don't be—it wasn't your fault. I wasn't moaning, just stating a fact. I'm sorry, Creena . . .'

'She won't mind,' Mike said airily. 'She's used to it—what with Dad and Dennis . . .'

There was a long silence and then Bart said in a startled voice, 'Oh yes, of course, Dennis . . .'

Creena could have slapped her brother. Of all the tactless stupid things to do—why drag Dennis into it? Especially as he knew very well she was not in love with Dennis . . .

Or was she—and just unwilling to admit it? Could Audrey be right?

Bart was driving fast and yet it seemed an endless time before he turned into a winding drive at Mike's directions. It was a big rambling old house surrounded by a wilderness of trees and shrubs. The Calendars lived there but although Creena knew them she had never been to their house before.

A tall thin boy of Mike's age whom Creena recognized vaguely came hurrying out and in a moment, Bart, Mike and Sandy had disappeared round the back of the house.

Creena was left in the car, wondering what to do. She knew that Bart had instantly forgotten her—that there was no way in which she could help. She sat on and on, glancing at the shabby old house, meeting the startled eyes of an African housegirl who appeared for a moment on the stoep and then vanished. At last Creena felt restless and got out of the car, following the path the others had taken.

Just round the corner of the house, she paused, her throat contracting painfully. She could guess what had happened. Bart was on his knees by a small boy of seven or eight, his arms round him, as he talked earnestly. On the ground before them, was the white body of a terrier. Even from that distance, Creena could see the distorted face of the small boy as he struggled with tears.

Slowly Creena returned to the car and patiently waited until finally Bart came along alone. His face was grave, his apology curt.

'Sorry to be so long. Wanted to get the burial over and done with—unfortunate the boys' parents are out for the day . . .' He reversed the car and started to drive along the winding overgrown road-way. 'Dog had been bitten some time before the kids discovered it,' he went on tersely. 'Sandy had done his best— pity they hadn't a snake-bite outfit handy—get tired of telling people it's a good investment— might have been that little kid . . .' Creena was watching his hands tighten on the steering wheel. How tense he was, his knuckles were white. 'It's a hell of a position to be in,

Creena,' Bart went on, his voice quietly explosive. 'To have to tell a kid of that age that it's too late—that his beloved friend is dead. To Jeremy this is the end of everything—he's too young to know that Nature decrees wisely that in time we forget everything, no matter how terrible the sense of loss is at the time. Mike is a good lad, Creena—he and Sandy are taking care of Jeremy. He's a brave little kid. Took it very well . . .'

Bart was talking almost as if to himself. From her place by his side, Creena could only see his profile, see the way his mouth tightened every now and then. She was surprised when he suddenly turned to her and said:

'Why? Tell me, Creena, why must a kid like that lose his only friend? The boy isn't a strong lad, Mike was telling me he doesn't make friends easily—his parents leave him more or less to his own devices. They are both artists, both very casual in their relationships with their children—Jeremy's whole love was centred on that dog. Why . . . why . . . why . . .' He pounded one fist on the steering wheel. In a moment he had himself under control and smiled down at the pretty girl by his side apologetically. 'Sorry about that, Creena. I ought to be used to death by now—unfortunately . . .' He sighed, relaxing his hands, stretching his fingers slowly as he went on: 'I'm afraid I can't acquire that necessary acceptance of death. Every time I lose a patient—whether it be human or animal—I wonder if I have left something undone—if it could be my fault . . .'

'Oh, Bart,' Creena said, fighting the longing to put her hand on his, to comfort him. 'I'm sure you did your best.'

He smiled at her humorously. 'I know I did, Creena, but it might have been a pretty poor best. There is so much to learn, to remember . . . sometimes . . .' He sighed again. 'Sometimes I almost wish I had never taken up medicine. Perhaps Mother is right—I'm too imaginative. Too soft . . .'

Creena swivelled round to look at him. 'Don't talk nonsense, Bart,' she said crossly. 'That's . . . that's . . . ridiculous. Just because you are compassionate and understanding. Maybe'—She sought for the right words and paused for a moment—'Maybe it makes it harder for you but it's certainly much better for your patients.'

He looked almost absurdly pleased. 'You really think so?' Was there a wistful note in his voice? Did this strong, self-possessed man—was this impressive, confident, good man actually asking for her opinion? Wanting her praise, her encouragement? This was a new slant to him—was there a weakness here? A need to be assured occasionally that he was doing all right? To Creena, it gave added charm to this fascinating man. Before he had seemed so impersonal—like a tower of strength. To know that he suffered from the same weaknesses as herself—to know that he need someone, gave her considerable joy.

'Oh, Bart,' she said impulsively. 'Of course I think so. Everyone says what a wonderful doctor you are—what confidence they have in you—how much they like you—how glad they are you have come here.'

'Why . . . why, Creena . . .'

She saw that he was embarrassed, almost confused. A dull red filled his cheeks, turning the tips of his ears bright red.

They were driving along her road by now. She was sorry the little outing was over. Impulsively she asked him to stay to supper.

'There's a good film at the bioscope . . .'

He turned carefully in over the cattle trap, stopped the car and looked down at her. Suddenly it was as if a curtain had fallen down over his face. Those moments in which he had spoken so confidingly were gone. He was once again the woman-fearer, the impersonal Dr. Darling who knew how to put young women in their place.

'I'm afraid I can't thank you.' His voice was suddenly stiff and cold. 'I have other plans for tonight. Sorry the afternoon had such a dismal ending,' he went on still stiffly.

She slid out of the car, feeling as if she had been slapped.

'Not at all,' she said with equal coolness. 'It

was not your fault. Good-bye . . .'

She walked up the steps to the house, her back like a poker, completely unaware of the fact that the man in the car was staring after her almost hungrily, fighting the desire to race after her, to hold her close, telling himself again and again that he must remember that she was unofficially engaged to Dennis Tyson. Dennis, himself, had told him so just before he left for Johannesburg. It was something he must remember, Bart told himself sternly, even if he failed to understand how a girl like Creena could love a man like Tyson. Love was a strange thing . . .

CHAPTER EIGHT

Creena was alone in the house when Dennis drove up. His low-slung sports car swung over the cattle trap and he parked it beneath the wattle trees, glancing up towards the house almost as if expecting to see a figure come flying down the stairs to welcome him.

Creena was sitting alone on the stoep, tense and unhappy. At first she had been glad when her father had gone off to play golf and her mother walked down the lane to tea with old Mrs. Abercrombie. Mike and Norma were both out with their friends and she had the house to herself. She knew that she must expect Dennis some time that day but so much depended on what time they left Johannesburg. If it was true that Mrs. Crampton had gone to fetch him, they would not leave until later. Dennis usually liked to leave the big golden city in the early hours of the morning, getting away early before he had to face the great mass of traffic taking workers into the city. Vaguely she heard the car but she was so busily thinking that at first it did not ring a bell in her mind. She was telling herself for the thousandth time that there was no need to feel this panic—that no one could make her marry Dennis, that she could just ignore her mother's coy looks and hints, that she was a free agent and that she only had to tell Dennis that she did not love him.

'Creena,' Dennis's warm excited voice broke into her thoughts.

Dimly she saw him come towards her—she stood up and the next moment was in his arms, his mouth hard against hers. It took her a few seconds to struggle and stand away from him. 'Dennis—I didn't hear you . . .'

He laughed. 'I must admit I was a bit hurt because you didn't come hurtling down to meet me. Missed me, honey?'

His arm still round her, he perched on the arm of her chair, dropping a kiss every now and then on the top of her head, on her neck, her bare arm.

She felt hot and confused, wishing he would

move away, that she could look at him. That fleeting second had disturbed her—was this the handsome man she had thought of so much? With whom she had gone out for three years, about whom she had occasionally dreamed? This man with the sleek dark hair, the small tight mouth, the dark intolerant impatient eyes.

'How is your arm?' she asked and moved a little way away from him.

As if conscious of the slight rebuff yet refusing to admit it had occurred, Dennis moved away from her, going to sit in another chair. He flexed his arm slowly.

'Much better . . .'

'I see it is out of a sling.' Creena was thinking wildly. If only she could keep the conversation going—keep him off the subject of loving her.

Dennis nodded. 'Oh, yes—it's fine but not quite right yet. I've got to have massage and exercises and all that tommyrot.' His voice was impatient. 'Muscles are a bit queer—I haven't proper control of my hand.' He scowled down at the hand in question. 'Damned annoying—means I can't do surgery.'

'Lucky you have Bart.' Creena said, little knowing what she was starting.

Dennis's face turned an ugly red. 'Darling? That . . .' He swallowed and she watched his Adam's apple jerking. 'I've a few things to say to him. Way he's been behaving. Mrs.

Crampton is pretty fed-up with him, I can tell you,' Dennis went on his voice changing again, to triumph this time. 'We'll be throwing him out just as soon as—'

'As soon as?' she echoed, feeling the chill fear creep down her spine.

Dennis shrugged. 'As soon as we can get another doctor. If only Mrs. Crampton wasn't so . . .' He made an obvious effort to control himself. 'I know she is trying to do as much as possible with the money her husband left for the hospital but she expects us to do the impossible. You can't run that hospital with one doctor . . .'

'That's what Bart says . . .'

'Bart!' Dennis exploded. 'Just wait until I see him . . . he's just a mere locum but seems to think he's running the whole show. The way he has been interfering with . . .' He swallowed again. Looked round. 'Where are your old folk?'

'Out.'

He looked well pleased. He spread himself out in the chair, stretching his long legs, tilting the chair back a little. 'Good—I can talk plainly, then. What's all this I hear about new sterilization technique—new sanitary arrangements . . . drugs locked up. Matron is in a flat spin and in big trouble with Mrs. Crampton.'

'If Mrs. Crampton is so displeased with Dr. Darling,' Creena found herself saying angrily, 'why doesn't she dismiss him?'

Dennis leaned forward, his face ugly for a moment. 'Because we need him, that's why. Use your brains. We'd be in a real mess if there was just me—in this stupid state.' He waved his bad arm about angrily, 'And had to rely on your father and Dr. Pipp. They're both good men but old . . .' His face changed. 'Your father is a fine man, Creena,' he said, his voice calmer now, 'I admire him greatly but you must admit he can only relieve, help us out. We couldn't offer him a full-time position.'

'He wouldn't take it.' Creena snapped. 'He cannot work with Mrs. Crampton.'

'Who can?' Dennis demanded. 'Sometimes one has to . . .' He frowned. 'I suppose you've heard all about the new African doctor? It seems Bart bullied Mrs. Crampton into engaging one. I've never heard such tripe. Good money thrown away . . .'

Creena stifled a sigh. This was a side she knew well in Dennis. Inconsistent when it pleased him—who could imagine Mrs. Crampton allowing herself to be *bullied* by anyone? She had probably jumped at the idea—because you would not have to offer the same salary to an African doctor as you would to a European.

'Did he tell you about it?' Dennis demanded.

Creena shook her head. 'I don't often see him,' she said—which was the truth. Brief

126

moments in a hospital corridor—yesterday was the first time she and Bart had talked alone.

Dennis smiled. 'Good—stay away from him, girl, for you're mine. All mine . . .' He put out his hand and before she could move, captured hers. He pulled her towards him, holding her close, kissing her warmly, almost roughly. 'All mine. Have you set the wedding-day yet?'

She tried to escape but his arms were tightly clamped round her. 'Dennis . . .'

'We'll wait until my arm is right,' Dennis went on, his mouth wandering over her face as he ignored her attempts to break away. 'No hurry . . . hope the ring fits you . . .'

She made a fierce movement and broke free. 'Dennis,' she said almost desperately. 'I'm not going to—'

'Name the date?' he asked. He was breathing a little fast as he stared at her. 'Now don't say you're going to play hard to get?' he said angrily. 'We've been drifting towards this for three years and at last, I feel I am in a position to—'

'Dennis—please.' She put up her hands as he came towards her. 'Please stop it, Dennis. I don't—'

His face changed, the anger wiped out completely. Even his voice altered.

'I know, Creena, I'm going about this the wrong way. I'm sorry, darling. I'm always so impatient,' he said in a penitent voice. 'A girl like you needs wooing—with flowers, presents, soft lights and sweet music. Isn't that right, darling?' He smiled at her gently. 'I promise I won't rush you, honey. We'll just go on the way we have been but you'll know how I feel about you—you'll know that I'm just waiting for you to name the day . . . is that all right?'

Creena stared at him. She just could not believe it. This was a Dennis she had never seen before. A humble, pleading Dennis—a gentle kind Dennis. She felt more confused than ever. Were there sides to Dennis she had never glimpsed? Had she misjudged him? She had been prepared to do battle—to have a terrible quarrel with Dennis walking out in a fury and from then on, leaving her severely alone. She was totally unprepared for this new Dennis.

'I . . . I . . .' She did not know what to say.

Dennis smiled. 'That's all right, then, honey. Let's just drop the subject and drift on as we have been doing—but remember that from now on, it is up to you. As soon as you are ready, just the name the day . . . Okay?'

Before she could answer they heard the galloping of horses . . . Creena hurried outside, Mike and his friends were riding up to the paddock. Mike waved his arm vigorously.

'It'll soon be the gymkhana,' Creena said, seizing the opportunity to avoid a direct answer. If Dennis's way meant that they could slowly drift apart without any unpleasantness, then it suited her beautifully. Klomati was too small a place to go on living in if you quarrelled violently with someone—you were bound to meet them every day and it could be most embarrassing.

Dennis shrugged his broad shoulders. He looked very smart in his dark suit. He must have rushed straight here, not even bothering to change into his usual tropical suit. 'Afraid I'm out of it this year . . .'

'Pity,' Creena said cryptically, aware that he was looking at her. 'I wonder if Bart can ride . . .' she said.

'I very much doubt it—he hasn't got the sort of background that leads you to expect him to ride,' Dennis said. 'He doesn't play cricket— very poor golf.'

'He is a wonderful swimmer,' Creena said.

Dennis stared at her, narrowing his eyes. 'Don't tell me you are carrying the torch for Darling.'

She felt her cheeks burning. 'Of course not,' she said indignantly. 'Besides he isn't a woman's man—he just isn't interested in us . . .'

'Probably scared of getting caught,' Dennis said with a quick laugh. 'Meg had better pull up her socks. She's got her claws in him all right . . .'

'Hi . . .' Mike said cheerfully as he walked in. His face changed as he saw Dennis . . . 'I didn't know you were back already,' he went on, his voice hostile.

Dennis looked at him and his mouth tightened. 'Yes, I am—and about time too, I'm beginning to think,' he added grimly. He turned to Creena. 'Come and see me off, honey. I've lots to do. Haven't even unpacked yet . . .'

They walked down to the parked car. As he slid behind the steering wheel, Dennis took hold of Creena's hand. He smiled at her. 'Look, honey, I've promised not to rush you but that doesn't mean I'm not going to see a lot of you. Tomorrow night—dinner at *Jackie's?* Okay?'

She could think of no excuse. 'Okay,' she agreed and walked slowly back to the house. She felt uneasy, worried, annoyed with herself. She had intended to tell him firmly that she did not love him, that there was no future for them to share. Instead Dennis had whipped the ground away from beneath her feet and she was in the same difficult situation. Why hadn't she had the strength to break the whole thing off properly? Now it was a real mess— now she had agreed to go out with him and everyone would say . . .

Mike was sprawled in an arm-chair in the lounge, the dogs around him, all panting and their tails wagging in greeting as Creena walked in. Mike was tilting a bottle of Coke down his mouth. He grimaced at his sister.

'That drip back,' he said sourly. 'Why don't you send him packing.'

Creena sank down on to the couch, her hand going out instinctively to Rudi, who came to lie by her side. 'I don't know,' she said, sighing. 'I meant to but . . .'

'You're just weak,' Mike said disgustedly. 'Look, Sis—you either love a guy or you don't. So—you don't love this creep. Tell him so and let him get out. It's as simple as that.'

'Simple,' Creena said. She stood up, staring down at her brother in his khaki shorts and shirt, sprawled in the chair, so assured that life was easy. 'Nothing is ever simple,' she said passionately.

Mike drained the bottle and put it on the floor. He stretched his long thin body. 'Boy— are you a mess. Now why couldn't you have fallen for someone like Bart?' he demanded.

Creena gave him a disgusted look and walked out of the room. In her bedroom, she stretched out on the bed, going back over the conversation. Why—oh why—hadn't she told Dennis firmly that she was not in love with him, had no intention of marrying him—and that she would never go out with him again? Simple—as Mike said. And yet somehow—she could not have done it. Not with this new strangely gentle Dennis. Somehow something had stopped her. Now she was involved all over again.

131

CHAPTER NINE

Just how badly involved she was, she did not realize until the following day when she drove to the hospital. It was a perfect day—cloudless blue sky, the hospital garden full of flowers, deep blue larkspur, great bushes of blue and pink hydrangeas, rose bushes with deep red roses, stocks, white-scented nicotina plants. The mountains rose on every side—the river was a silver finger in the distance.

She went inside to her small office and had barely taken off the cover of the typewriter when Dennis was there.

'Hi—honey,' he said in his loud, carrying voice. 'Gosh—is it good to be back and near you again . . .'

Creena looked up startled. Dennis was standing very near her, his arm round her shoulders. 'Dennis,' she said softly in a shocked voice. 'Someone will hear you.'

It was so unlike him. In the past, he had been the one who cautioned her about letting anyone know about them; today, he had suddenly changed.

Now he laughed and rubbed his cheek against hers. 'I know, honey. We're not to say anything until you give me the word but all the same, I don't care who knows how I feel about you . . .'

132

'Please, Dennis,' she whispered, her cheeks aflame. Voices carried clearly down the corridor—the Matron—the Sisters—even the patients might hear. 'Look, Dennis,' she began desperately. 'I don't—'

'Honey,' he interrupted her. 'Afraid I can't stay now. I've got to go and do battle . . .'

'Battle?'

'Yes,' he said almost gaily. 'Do battle with our darling . . .'

'Our darling.' Again she echoed his words, not understanding. Then suddenly she knew what he meant and her cheeks were dyed with dismayed colour. 'Dennis . . . don't speak so loudly,' she whispered unhappily. 'He might hear you.'

'I hope he does—see you later . . .' Dennis said and walked off jauntily.

It was a day like any other and yet it was completely different. Booking appointments, telling callers that Dr. Tyson was back and available, having the nurses pop in to see her for a moment's chat, even plump, red-faced old Matron who was shaking like an aspen leaf as she forecast the terrible scene there was going to be when the two doctors finally met— through all these moments ran a thread of suspense. Janice said frankly that Dennis was right—they needed another European doctor not an African. Meg's view was that Bart was right.

'We're always overworked in the African

part,' she said worriedly. 'Dr. Darling spends a lot of time there that he can ill spare. A good African doctor would be worth his weight in gold.'

The walking European patients dropped in as well. Mrs. Isipin being one of them unfortunately. She was still having trouble with her ankle and there was talk of sending her down to Johannesburg.

Creena went on typing furiously, just looking up now and then, but it didn't worry Mrs. Isipin. Her rasping acid-touched voice droned on and on. She didn't know what the hospital was coming to—surely it was time they had a senior doctor able and competent enough to take a firm stand—and the doctors hadn't been near her that day—and it was rather disgraceful when you thought of what you paid . . .

In despair Creena slowed down her hands and looked at the beak-nosed woman. Was she really the unhappy mixed-up woman Bart seemed to think she was—or just a bitter woman who liked to hurt others?

'I'm afraid there has been an emergency, Mrs. Isipin,' Creena said with frigid politeness. 'Out at the Mill, several people were badly injured. Dr. Darling has gone out there and I know that Dr. Tyson is very busy with some patients who were rushed in.'

'The African wards, I suppose,' Mrs. Isipin sniffed.

'They are also humans,' Creena said quietly.

Mrs. Isipin looked at her. 'I'm not suggesting they are not,' she said tartly. 'But there happens to be a vast difference between the shilling they pay and the heavy medical expenses I am expected to shoulder.'

'I'll contact Dr. Tyson,' Creena said, reaching for the telephone.

'Oh, no—no . . .' Mrs. Isipin said quickly. 'Don't bother him. In any case, I prefer to continue having Dr. Darling as he knows my case.'

As the day wore on wearily, Creena noticed something a little disturbing. At least, it might have been disturbing had she still been in love with Dennis. All the patients seemed to want to wait for Bart—those who telephoned said they wanted to see Bart as he knew about their particular case. Somehow she had expected everyone to rush back to Dennis—whom they knew so well and had known for so long. She wondered what Dennis would say about it.

She had left the hospital before Bart returned from the Mill. It was Mike's birthday and they were having a braavleis up near the race course. There were a crowd of young people and a few friends of the Halls and the smoke of the fires rose slowly in the star-spangled sky and the scent of roasting steaks drifted on the breeze. Creena stayed near her father and he asked her why she was so silent.

On a sudden impulse, Creena confided in

135

him. 'Dennis says he is going to stop Bart making the alterations he plans—that he won't have the African doctor and . . .'

Dr. Hall tapped out his pipe and leaned back in his deck-chair. His face was easily seen in the bright light from the blazing fire. He smiled.

'Bart can take care of himself,' he said lazily. 'You don't need to worry about him, Creena. Or—he paused significantly—'is it Dennis you are worrying about?'

Creena swallowed. 'I'm worried about the hospital. There's a horrible atmosphere there at the moment. Everyone tense and—'

'The hospital was always like that—to me,' her father said. His voice changed. 'Why—Bart—good to see you . . .'

Creena swung round and there was Bart himself. He looked tired but very big and strong as he stood there in his thin suit.

'Mike asked me to drop in so I thought I'd come along . . .'

'Doc,' Mike was shouting. 'Come over here and see what we've got . . .'

Bart smiled at Creena and her father, shrugged a little, and walked round the fires to join the group of young men who had a mandolin, a ukelele, a couple of mouth organs and were starting a sing-song.

Dr. Hall yawned. 'He must be dead. When I called the hospital at seven, he was still out at the Mill. I wonder what happened out there.'

Creena had all the details. A bulldozer had got out of control—running down a mountain slope—pinning several Africans under it. Falling trees uprooted as a result had injured others. 'No one killed . . .'

Her father sighed. 'Might be better if they had died. Life is pretty tough for a crippled African though I will say they are good to their sick in these parts. I don't know about you, Creena, but your mother and I are going home. We're getting a little old for this sort of thing.'

Creena laughed. 'I think I'll come as well. Most of Mike's friends are too young for me . . .'

She was gathering rugs and baskets with her mother when Bart came up.

'Going, Creena?' he asked and sounded quite disappointed. For a moment, she was tempted to change her mind. But already he had turned away and was speaking to her father. 'I'm going to live up at the hospital in future, sir. I'm having that cottage by the side of the T.B. ward . . .'

Dr. Hall's eyes were twinkling. 'So you'll be right on the spot, eh?' He chuckled. 'Very clever. I bet the old girl is charging you rent?'

'Oh, yes,' Bart said cheerfully. 'Actually I don't mind. I hate hotel life and I'm quite a good cook . . .'

'You'll get a cook-boy, of course,' Creena's mother said.

'Perhaps,' Bart said and laughed. 'Anyhow I don't mind the move.'

'Actually,' Dr. Hall said slowly. 'It's quite a good idea. It's awkward at times when an emergency comes in during the night and you have to be dragged out of the hotel. Now you'll just be able to slide out of bed and be on the spot.'

'I wonder Dennis hasn't been given that cottage before,' Mrs. Hall said suddenly. 'It seems strange to me. After all, he can't really enjoy being a lodger at the Keeton . . .'

'He isn't—any longer,' Bart said. 'He's going to live at Mrs. Crampton's.'

There was a sudden silence. Creena was startled. It seemed odd that Dennis hadn't told her. 'But what on earth—' Her father said abruptly.

Bart's face was grave. 'I understand that Mrs. Crampton suffers from a tired heart and is very alarmed about her general health. Maybe she thinks this will protect her.'

'She'll be lucky if he's in any night before 2 am.,' Dr. Hall said.

'Bill,' Mrs. Hall said in a shocked voice. 'That's not quite fair to Dennis . . .'

'Well—I mustn't keep you,' Bart said politely. 'I'll just stay here for an hour or so—it was nice of Mike to invite me—and then I'm hitting the hay.'

Sudden compassion swept Creena. They were all making use of Bart—and he was too

138

fine a man to be given such treatment. 'You must be dead tired,' she said warmly.

Bart looked at her and in the firelight there was something strange about his expression. 'Not more than usual,' he said curtly. 'A doctor gets conditioned to fatigue.'

In the car with her parents, Creena sat silently, listening to them arguing. Her father took her view—that Bart was being exploited; her mother said that Bart would never be the doctor Dennis was, and Dr. Hall said he thanked God for that . . . In the end, Creena retreated mentally and went over the short conversation. Why had he snapped her head off? It had simply been a sympathetic question or statement of hers. Logically he must be very tired. No matter how conditioned a doctor was—he got tired so why deny it?

As she undressed and slid into bed, she thought of the following day with a feeling of dread. What would happen when Dennis and Bart did 'battle'? Who would win? And who would get hurt? How would Mrs. Crampton react? After all, she had agreed to having an African doctor—nothing Dennis could say could alter that. Unless Dennis had made Mrs. Crampton review the whole situation? It seemed so odd that Dennis should be going to stay in Mrs. Crarnpton's house. How would he like it? He always said she was so difficult to get on with—so exhausting in her demands. Maybe he thought it was worth the price—that this way, he could influence her more, Creena thought and was instantly ashamed of herself. Dennis was not like that!

CHAPTER TEN

It was strange how much she had dreaded the fight between Bart and Dennis and yet when it happened, it all seemed to fizzle out. Creena never learned the details of what happened but later that morning, Bart stopped by her desk. He wore his white coat and his thick fair hair was rumpled.

'Dr. Roda Cindi will be arriving by the bus, Miss Hall.' His voice was formal but that did not hurt her, for Mrs. Isipin and Matron were talking in the hall and it could have been because of that. 'I'd be grateful if you would arrange transport for her to be met. She is going to stay with the Dhlaminis.' Israel Dhlamini was an African Civil Servant and lived just outside Klomati.

'Roda,' Creena repeated. 'A woman doctor?'

Bart nodded curtly. 'She has an excellent record and will undoubtedly be a great asset to the hospital.' His voice was loud and firm and without another word, he strode away.

Matron and Mrs. Isipin stopped talking and came to stand near Creena.

'So Dennis lost the fight,' Mrs. Isipin said gleefully.

Matron's round, reddish face looked perturbed. 'I really don't know—I think, actually, it was Mrs. Crampton who insisted that we need an African doctor . . .'

Creena ignored them, telephoning for the African orderly whom they used occasionally as a chauffeur, giving him instructions, and when she had finished, she was relieved to see that Mrs. Isipin and Matron had moved away.

She stared at her typewriter for a long while. How would Dennis react? Would he see this as a defeat? Would it make him hate Bart more than ever? And a woman doctor, too. Dennis had always loudly declared he had no use for female medicos. Involuntarily Creena smiled. Mike had seized the opportunity to later say sarcastically that Dennis was probably scared lest the woman doctor be cleverer than he was! The family had naturally commented on Mike's treatment of the English language— Mrs. Hall had said that Dennis was a fine doctor—Norma had looked as though she wanted to say something and thought the better of it, and Dr. Hall had said that many men doctors had a *thing* about women doctors. It was strange how divided the family was in their opinion of Dennis—two members on each side. Nervously, Creena awaited her first sight of Dennis. Was he going to be in a terrible temper?

Her fears were groundless. She was eating sanwiches for lunch, sitting under the great oak tree whose spreading branches offered welcome shade from the great heat of the sun. Usually she went home to lunch but that day her mother was going to be out on one of her twice-monthly sketching trips with some friends, and her father was playing golf with a visiting V.I.P. and then going to lunch at the Residency. As she was sitting there, a little way away from the groups of Africans who were squatting on the ground, dipping fingers into bowls of mealie-pap, with children running around and laughing excitedly, Creena was far away. She was rehearsing a conversation she was going to have with Dennis in which she would tell him very firmly that much as she liked him, she could never marry him. It was getting more embarrassing than ever—in the hospital, everyone seemed to take it for granted that in a matter of a few months, she would be Mrs. Tyson. Even Janice, whom everyone knew loved Dennis to desperation, had congratulated her and had, when Creena vehemently denied it, merely smiled knowingly. So obviously Dennis was telling everyone that they were to be married but that Creena was being *difficult.*

Suddenly Dennis was walking across the grass to her, flinging himself down by her side, taking her hand. 'Hi—honey,' he greeted her.

She tried to take her hand away, very

conscious that the windows of the European wards faced this way. She saw, to her amazement, that Dennis was in a very good humour. He soon explained why.

'It means I need have nothing more to do with the African wards,' he said cheerfully. 'Mrs. Crampton says I am needed more on the European side. Darling can keep an eye on this African girl and when the new doctor arrives, he will automatically have to do the same. As you know, I have little patience with these people who keep getting their heads bashed in when they drink too much and who come whining with each little ache and pain demanding huge bottles of *mooti* for their shilling. Darling is a crank—he wastes valuable time there . . . but then it isn't for long.'

'Have you a new doctor lined up?' Creena asked, managing at last to take possession of her own hand.

Dennis stretched luxuriously. He glanced over at the crowds of Africans, colourful in their bright red, yellow and blue dresses. He frowned. 'You pick a noisy spot for your lunch hour . . .'

'The shade is lovely and I'm so used to them that I don't hear the noise. Have you got a doctor?' she repeated.

He shook his head. 'Several applied but they all want larger salaries than Mrs. Crampton is prepared to pay. That's the snag . . .' He tore out a blade of grass and began to twist it into knots. This made Creena look at his hands. Long thin fingers, square hands. Strong hands. The blade of grass suddenly snapped. Dennis looked up at her swiftly and for a moment she was frightened at the cruelty in his eyes. 'I'd like to do that with Bartholomew Darling . . .' He was speaking softly. 'Why I was fool enough ever to send that wire to him . . .'

'He's been useful.'

Dennis scowled for a moment and then his face cleared. 'Yes, he's been useful and it isn't for ever.' He smiled at her. 'Decided which month yet?'

'Which month?' Creena echoed and then understood. She leaned towards him. 'Dennis—I want to talk to you . . .' she began gravely.

He was on his feet. 'Sorry—have to go. Just saw Matron waving to me . . .'

He walked rapidly across the grass and she knew he had lied to her. Why had he suddenly left her like that? Had he an idea that she was going to tell him she did not love him? Was he determined not to let her do so?

Why was everyone so determined to marry her to Dennis? If only people would leave them alone.

Later that day she met the new African doctor. A slim intelligent-looking girl with dark glowing eyes and a disciplined mouth. She talked very formally and there was a wary look in her eyes. Yes, she said, she had met all the doctors. Dr. Darling was most kind . . . she understood that Dr. Tyson was on the European side. There was a note in her voice that made Creena believe that Dr. Cindi had been told that Dr. Tyson and the secretary were going to be married—though why they should . . . Or was it just that she was getting sensitive, she wondered.

That night she went with Dennis to one of Mrs. Andrew's musical evenings. The crowded but beautifully furnished room was packed with people, drinking coffee, falling into silence as Mrs. Andrew put on a long-playing record and made a sign that everyone be still. It was beautiful music but Creena felt restless and in the interval when fresh coffee and cakes were served, she wandered round the room and found herself next to Mrs. Crampton.

A wizened, wrinkled little old woman with a curving nose, her eyes were little black beads. Her thin heavily-veined hand rested on Creena's arm for a moment as she smiled: 'I am so glad about you and Dennis . . .' she said softly. 'He badly needs someone like you.'

Creena felt her face burning. 'But Mrs. Crampton . . .' she began.

Dennis was suddenly there. Had he been on the lookout for just such an incident? His arm was lightly round her shoulders as he smiled at Mrs. Crampton.

'Now . . . now . . .' he scolded. 'I told you it was a secret. I mustn't rush Creena, she wants

145

to be very sure . . .'

'And quite right, too,' Mrs. Crampton said tartly. 'You've been a very wild young man and no girl in her senses would—'

'Please,' Dennis said, giving her a smile. 'I'm no longer wild. See how you have tamed me?' He turned to Creena. 'Isn't it good of Mrs. Crampton to give me such a lovely home? She really spoils me. It reminds me of my own home—before my parents died, I mean.'

'Yes, poor boy. It's hard to be young and alone in the world,' Mrs. Crampton said. She straightened the skirt of her black lace frock, her face wistful. 'I think, though, it may be harder to be old and alone in the world. That is why it is so good of Dennis to come and look after me.' Her hand fluttered to the region of her heart as she smiled at Creena. 'I feel so much safer nowadays.'

Mrs. Andrew tapped imperatively on the radiogram. 'Take your seats, please . . .'

Dennis grinned at Creena and whispered. 'Like a ruddy sergeant-major, isn't she, and this is supposed to be fun . . .'

'Why do you come?' she whispered back as they took their seats.

'Don't be a clot, honey,' Dennis said softly in her ear.

She knew what he meant. Why did it disgust her now—and yet, in the past, she had looked on his social-climbing, his carefully applied charm as being quite natural in a young ambitious doctor.

Driving her home later, he startled her by saying abruptly: 'Are you playing fair with me, honey?'

In the darkness she turned to stare at him. 'What do you mean?'

'Just that . . . that I seem to have lost most of my private patients, these days.'

She caught her breath. She had wondered how long it would be before he realized how many people had turned to Bart.

'You were away so long, Dennis, and . . . and I think they feel that it is better to stick to one doctor and—'

'You'll have to think up a better reason than that, honey,' he said mildly. 'I've been here longer than Darling and I'll be here when he goes so the logical answer is for them to return to me just as soon as I'm back.'

There was silence as she stared ahead at the wide white blades of light that pierced the darkness of the winding mountain road.

'It's difficult,' she said unhappily.

'Not difficult at all,' Dennis told her, still in that mild voice.

'Well, Bart can hardly turn them away . . .'

'Trust him not to do so—he's stolen them from me, that's what he's done. Deliberately . . .' Dennis's voice rose momentarily and then he lowered it. 'But you could help me, honey. Just say that Dr. Darling is too busy to see them—just that now Dr. Tyson has returned and as they are his patients . . . You could easily get them all back for me . . .'

'But Dennis—would that be—'

'Ethical?' He supplied the word with a laugh. 'Is Darling's conduct ethical, come to that?'

She was silent. She was certain that Bart had not deliberately enticed Dennis's patients away from him. So many people had remarked to her that in Dr. Darling's surgery you could relax, you had no feeling that he was impatient to get rid of you because of the queue waiting outside the door. It was true that Dennis had a brusque, rather unsympathetic manner with patients—unless they were going to be important to him. He had no use for what he termed *neurotics* and once he had sent a girl of seventeen away in tears because he had told her she was pretending to be ill just to get attention from a doctor. Creena knew she would never forget the day—the look on that girl's face, just as if she had been slapped. Nor was it true—for shortly afterwards, the girl had developed symptoms, been taken to Johannesburg by her indignant parents and later operated on for a small but benign tumour. No—Dennis might be a brilliant surgeon but as a G.P. he was too impatient. He demanded symptoms—he had no time for what he called imaginary woes. Now Bart was quite the opposite. He was always talking about psychosomatic medicine, about the need

148

to understand the patient's emotional background. He wasted what Dennis would call valuable time, just listening to the outpourings from the hearts of those who sought his help.

'I can count on you, honey?' Dennis asked abruptly as he turned the car in over the cattle trap and turned to her.

She was quick to act. In a moment, she had the car door open and was half-out. 'Thanks for taking me, Dennis,' she said quickly.

But he was not as easily outwitted. Ile caught her up as she walked up the twisting pathway—the stone steps were too dangerous in a dark night without a torch. He took her in his arms. 'Creena, honey . . .'

'Please, Dennis—I'm not in . . .' she began.

He kissed her and released her. 'In a romantic mood?' he teased. 'Maybe I'll have better luck next time.'

She heard his laughter as he left her and went back to his car. And again she had the strangest feeling that he knew what she was trying to do and was determined to give her no opportunity.

Indoors she undressed slowly. She had avoided giving Dennis a direct answer but she knew in her heart that no matter what he said, she would never deliberately take a patient away from Bart. It wouldn't be . . . it wouldn't be *right*.

It was strange as the days passed. just as

149

when Bart had come to the small town, the excitement at the presence of a new doctor had swept through it like a bush fire—so now suddenly there was displeasure and discontent with Dennis. Creena came across it in a thousand small ways. For some reason, Dennis was in most people's black books. At the hospital there were murmurings that he was leaving too much to Dr. Darling—there was talk of the time he could not be found when someone was in labour and that Dr. Darling had been called in at the last moment and that Dr. Tyson had been very angry about it. There was mention of a dog being badly injured in a car crash and someone said that Dr. Tyson had said it was only a dog and he had an appointment and the dog died. Well, as Creena's father said, the dog would probably have died anyhow but at least, Dennis could have done something.

The house seemed to seethe with suppressed undercurrents. Although her mother said nothing to her, Creena knew that she had been talking to Dennis and once Creena found her mother studying a book of designs for wedding-dresses! Norma took it for granted that there was to be a wedding and she seemed even more sulky than before. She told Creena emphatically that she was not going to be a bridesmaid and when Creena said there was to be no wedding, Norma looked very shocked and told her that she could not treat

Dennis like that! Mike came home with a new story each day and gleefully recounted them—to Norma's fury and their mother's dismay.

'Just why does Dennis have to live at Mrs. Crampton's?' Mike demanded one day. 'Everyone says he is sucking up to her in the hope that she will leave him everything.'

That was too much. Even in her new mood, Creena could not let that pass.

'Nonsense, Mike. She has relatives. Ailsa is her granddaughter . . . she probably has other children.'

Mike sprawled on the grass in the sun and Samson lay on top of him, gently chewing his ear while Mike scratched the dog's head. 'I wonder. Isn't she always moaning about being all alone and having no one to care for her . . .'

'She has a tired heart,' Creena told him severely. 'If you were old and frightened of your health and you could get a doctor to live in the house . . .'

'I'd run a mile if that doctor was Dennis,' Mike said cheerfully. He was watching Norma's plump face redden. 'Besides—whose word have we that she has a weak heart?'

'Mike,' his mother scolded. 'It's not funny to talk like—'

'Hey, Dad,' Mike asked as his father came out into the garden and sat down rather heavily on the swing chair. 'Is it true Mrs. Crampton has a weak heart?'

Creena noticed how her father hesitated.

'She hasn't actually a weak heart,' he said carefully. 'A tired one, perhaps. The trouble is that she is very concerned with her health and a frightened woman of her age could—'

'Do you think Dennis has to live there?' Mike demanded.

Dr. Hall sensed the tenseness in the atmosphere. He smiled.

'Isn't that his business?' he asked mildly. 'Personally I'd loathe it but if it makes the old woman any happier . . .'

At the hospital everything seemed to be running smoothly. If Dennis was planning to stop Bart's plans for improvement, he did not seem to be doing anything active about it. Except delaying their progress.

Meg came into the little office one day, her face white with anger.

'Why doesn't Bart do something about it?' she asked Creena.

'About what?' Creena asked carefully. There was another rumour going round that Bart and Meg were stepping out together but Creena paid little attention to it, remembering Bart's plan to get Meg to consent to her mother leading the kind of life that would make her happy, and not one that would make Meg look like a good daughter. Maybe Bart did go and see Meg's mother quite often but it could be . . .

'Bart got Mrs. Crampton to consent to build a new wing to the T.R. wards. Now there is

152

some hold-up—they're changing the architect
. . . it's all Dennis's doing. He's just jealous . . .'
Meg hissed in Creena's ear.

It could be true, Creena thought when she
was alone again. It could be Dennis's way to
outwit Bart, knowing that once Bart had gone,
he could do what he liked about it. Nearly
every day an application for the post of doctor
came in but invariably when Creena typed
Mrs. Crampton's replies, nothing followed.
Talking it over with her father, he said that
Mrs. Crampton would not be likely to get the
kind of doctor they needed for few men,
especially men with families, could afford to
accept the low salaries she offered.

'It's men like Bart we need,' her father said.
'Dedicated men.'

She was to hear the word again a few days
later. At last it was the day of the gymkhana. A
bright day with clouds gathering on the
horizon. A crowd had gathered at the race
course. On one side of the track were
hundreds of Africans—their dark faces
gleaming with excitement, their white teeth
flashing. Men in brightly coloured blankets
and strips of cotton material, many in smart
grey suits with hats; women in their gaudy
clothes and beads, their hair piled high, but an
equal number in bright cotton frocks, walking
around with yellow or red sunshades, many
wearing dark glasses. It was a curious scene,
and to Creena always fascinating, mixture of

the old world and the new but there was no doubt that they all loved to watch the horses with their riders as they raced past the crowd. The air was filled with laughter and chatter, the background of raucous music from the loudspeakers always there. On the other side of the track were the Europeans—a crowd had gathered.

The children's events were always first and many a parent's heart fluttered with fear as he or she watched their wonderful childen jumping or weaving their horses through the poles. Mike won two events and then Creena rode—Snow-White was a powerful horse who loved jumping and she sailed round the field easily. But she was not so clever when it came to winding in and out of the poles. All the same, Creena gave her a hug and a pat and put her in the adjoining paddock to graze.

Creena strolled to the track to watch the next race. Tent-pegging was always fascinating to watch. In her well-cut jodhpurs, her white silk shirt and shining boots, she looked very lovely although she was quite unaware of it. Her elfin face was eager as she watched excitedly and shouted praise, her slanting green eyes showed surprise as she looked up at the big man who suddenly came to stand by her side.

'You jumped well . . .' Bart said in his deep voice.

She laughed up at him. 'You mean Snow-

154

White jumped well. She's wonderful.'

He looked down at her. 'You all seem to enjoy riding so much that I'm beginning to wish I could . . .'

'I'll teach you,' Creena offered spontaneously.

He smiled again. 'Afraid I shan't be here long enough. I'm only a locum you know . . .' There was a strange note in his voice.

'I wish . . .' Creena began impulsively. She paused. They stared at one another for a moment. It was as if they were alone. Creena felt herself longing for the moment to continue for ever as she gazed into his eyes—and yet longing for it to be over because of the breathlessness that filled her. And then he moved, looking at Mike who galloped by, brandishing a sword.

'Pity Tyson can't ride—he must be disappointed,' he said, his voice flat and disapproving.

Creena's cheeks burned. Why must he always be like this? So friendly for a moment and then suddenly so distant.

'I don't think he really minds,' she said with equal coldness. 'Dennis is not very keen.'

Bart looked around. 'He isn't here?'

'No,' she said curtly. Why bother to explain to him that Dennis had gone to Nsingisi with Mrs. Crampton for some unknown reason.

Bart took a deep breath and turned to look at the girl by his side.

'When are you getting married? Mrs. Crampton appears to approve,' he said frostily. 'I gather she feels that it will help Tyson to settle down. She takes a keen interest in his welfare.'

'He is very good to her,' Creena said angrily.

Bart lifted his eyebrows. 'Granted. He is— very good to her. Perhaps she is right—you will do Tyson good . . . '

She swallowed. 'Look—you've always said a doctor shouldn't marry . . .'

'You misquote me,' he told her coldly. 'I said a dedicated doctor . . .'

Her face was burning hot. She hated him. 'You're so smug . . .' she told him fiercely. 'In any case, I'm not—'

There was a sudden cry over the field and Creena looked up. One of the riders was sprawled on the ground, the horse had fallen on top of him . . . Stewards were running and in a moment, Bart had vaulted the rail and was running as well, dropping to his knees as the horse was pulled off the crumpled body. In a moment there was the sound of a shot and the horse's legs gave a last convulsive shudder and Creena turned away feeling very sick, her hands to her face. The horse must have broken a leg . . . how awful.

'The boy's all right,' a voice said by her side. It was her father, his face white and concerned.

'Mike?' Creena gasped. 'It happened so

quickly—I wasn't looking . . .'

'No—Sandy. But he's all right—Bart is getting him to hospital—slight concussion and some bad bruises. Might be a rib broken or two . . . but nothing much.'

'The poor horse, Dad,' Creena gulped back tears.

'It wasn't much of a horse at the best of times,' her father said quietly. 'Mike told me that Sandy bought it for a song—it was getting on in years and actually he shouldn't have entered it for the animal wasn't fit.'

'Poor Sandy . . .'

Her father took her arm. 'Look, your mother and I are going home.'

'I think I'll go, too,' she said slowly. She did not want to have to speak to Bart again. 'I'll ride back . . .'

Riding Snow-White slowly home, she thought again of the conversation with Bart. Why was he always like that—so friendly and then suddenly so hostile and cold? And . . . and how very very conceited of him to consider himself a dedicated doctor and Dennis . . . Bart was impossible sometimes. It was just as well he would soon be leaving Klomati. The sooner the better . . .

CHAPTER ELEVEN

There was plenty to do at the hospital the next day. Creena always found that after a public holiday the work had piled up. She was immersed in accounts, letters, appointments to be booked when the African doctor asked if she could spare a moment.

Dr. Cindi's eyes were glowing warmly as she told Creena what she wanted. 'This child has cataract,' she said, looking down at the small African child she had by the hand. Creena recognized the child as one she had often seen at the out-patients with an aged crone of a granny. 'Dr. Darling wants you to contact Baragwanath Hospital and arrange for the child to go down there for an operation . . .'

Creena looked at the child whose eyes were constantly blinking and who looked around her vaguely. 'I'm so glad,' Creena said. 'Will they be able to cure her?'

Dr. Cindi's face was happy. 'The prognosis is very favourable. Afterwards the child will be sent home and in about eighteen months have to go back again for a second operation and then she will have to wear glasses but she will see . . .'

'How wonderful,' Creena said. Alone, as she wrote the necessary letter to the Hospital she thought of the number of times that child had

158

attended the clinic and how often Dennis must have seen her—had he never thought of this?

She asked him when, later, he drifted in, to sit on her desk and tease her. Dennis looked surprised. 'Sure I thought of it but it seemed to me just waste of time. I don't for one moment believe they will let the child return for a second operation and as for her wearing glasses—she just won't do it.'

But at least, Creena thought silently, we shall have done our best.

'There's a dance at the Cellar tonight,' Dennis said abruptly. 'Would you like to go?' he asked. Even as she hesitated, he stood up. 'Good—I'll pick you up at eight o'clock.' He smiled at her.

She was suddenly aware that he was in a very happy mood. 'You seem very pleased with life.'

'I am,' he said cheerfully. He ran a gentle finger along her nose. 'Mrs. Crampton and I yesterday had a very profitable outing— profitable, that is, to me.' He lowered his voice. 'She was making a new will. She doesn't want anyone to know so we went to her solicitor's house as if on a social visit.' His voice was triumphant. 'You see, Creena, it does pay to be patient.'

She looked at him, suddenly revolted. Was Mrs. Crampton leaving him money?

'She may not die for years,' she said bluntly.

Dennis looked shocked but his eyes were

twinkling. 'I should hope not, Creena. She's a tough old bird—but all the same, the hospital will be mine.'

'The hospital?' she said softly.

He nodded. 'Yes, entirely mine and a trustee fund with which to run it. Nice work— eh? Just think what could be done here . . .' He waved his hand vaguely and smiled at her. 'See you—honey.' He walked off jauntily and she stared after him. So that was what it was all for—all his charm, his patience, his solicitude for the old lady. So that he could inherit the hospital . . . so that he could have power. She made up her mind. That night, at the dance, she would tell him the truth. That she did not love him, had never loved him, and had no intention at all of marrying him. She would make a complete breakaway—make it clear to him.

It is funny how easy it is to plan and how difficult to carry those plans out. That night at the gaily decorated Cellar under the Carlton Hotel, Creena found herself part of a crowd. About half a dozen couples teamed up together and danced in turn with one another. In a way, it was nice for it enabled her to keep away from too many quiet intimate moments with Dennis—on the other hand, it was annoying for she had planned to go outside with him and tell him the truth, bluntly, that she could never marry him, or *name the day* as he liked to put it.

She was dancing with Bob Hamilton when they saw Bart. He looked so very handsome, Creena thought, as she stared at the tall, broad man, immaculate in his dinner jacket, his thick fair hair smoothed down, his face calm. He was dancing with Rosalie Pipp, who was gazing up into his eyes soulfully.

Rosalie was very pretty, Creena thought. Ash-blonde hair, a frail look, scarlet voluptuous mouth, lovely little figure. She danced well, too. Creena had been told, and in the arms of the big man, she looked like a piece of Dresden china.

Bob was also watching. He smiled down at Creena. 'Have you heard Dr. Pipp is going to America?'

Creena was surprised. 'No, I hadn't. Isn't Rosalie going as well?'

'No. It seems it is something to do with a medical convention. Dr. Pipp wrote some thesis and has been invited to lecture. All expenses paid but he can't afford to pay for Rosalie as well. She is very browned off about it. That's probably why she is making eyes at Darling—to make her husband jealous.'

'But Bart wouldn't . . .' Creena said, shocked.

'Of course he wouldn't,' Bob said, swinging her round. 'But Rosalie doesn't know that—yet.'

'How's Audrey?' Creena said, a sudden desire to change the subject filling her. 'She came back and then went off again. Where is she now?'

'My cousin Audrey is unpredictable,' Bob said laughing. 'She's in Durban at the moment, taking a course in modelling. She talks of going to Paris.'

'Isn't she lucky,' Creena said, sighing a little. The music had stopped for a moment and she stood by Bob's side, tall, slim in her green flared silk frock, her red-gold hair brushed up to a little knot on top of her head, her eyes thoughtful.

'Is she?' Bob asked a little bitterly. 'I'd wager Audrey would swop the lot for the chance of having a family life like yours . . .'

But Creena was not listening. She was staring across the dance floor at Bart and he was looking back at her. His face grave, his eyes had a question. She had never danced with him. She wondered if he would ask her for one. What would it be like to be in his arms? To be held close to his heart?

And then he moved abruptly, bending his head to hear what Rosalie Pipp was saying as she smiled at him. Creena turned away, too, aware that Bob had said something but unable to remember it.

'I'll be glad when she's back,' she said. 'I miss her.'

'I didn't think you had time to miss anyone' Bob said with a whimsical look. 'Isn't your time taken up by that gallant cavalier—

Dennis?'

'Oh—Dennis,' Creena said vaguely and wondered why Bob looked at her so strangely.

Bart did not ask her to dance that evening though she waited tensely for him to do so. He danced with many girls and seemed to be avoiding Rosalie Pipp. Creena was having the last dance of the evening with Dennis when he began to laugh. She looked at him inquiringly.

'Just thinking what a fool Bartholomew Darling is,' he said. He always gave Bart his full name—making it sound ludicrous. 'He's been snubbing Rosalie Pipp all evening and she's mad as blazes with him. He'll live to rue the day—you see if he doesn't. Rosalie isn't a good enemy to make.'

'I don't suppose he meant to snub her . . .'

'Didn't he?' Dennis was laughing again. 'Well, I don't know, honey. I really don't know but when a pretty woman asks a man to take her out into the moonlight and he refuses—it seems mighty like a snub to me.'

'How do you know?' Creena asked, staring up at him. He was very good-looking with his classic features and his dark eyes.

'Because she told me so. She extended the invitation to me and I—'

'Took it?' Creena asked.

Dennis tightened his arm round her. 'But of course I did—a chance like that was too good to pass up. But you needn't be jealous—she bores me to tears.'

'I'm not jealous,' Creena said indignantly. 'Dennis, I must talk—'

It was as if he had not heard her. 'Would you mind if I gave Mrs. Pipp a lift home?' he asked. 'Seems she came with a party but they left early. I said I knew you wouldn't mind. We can drop you off on the way.'

'Of course I don't mind,' Creena said stiffly. It saved her from Dennis's love-making; on the other hand, it meant she would have no chance to talk to him alone. And she very badly wanted to get that final scene over and to have nothing more to do with him. Somehow she must make an opportunity. The trouble was that they had to be alone and with no danger of anyone interrupting them. Perhaps if she suggested they went for a drive . . .

It was as if Dennis was on the alert for the days passed and no chance to be alone with him came up. True he visited her home—true he took her out to dinner once but he brought a friend along in the car to meet Creena so that they were not alone the whole evening. And it seemed to Creena as if public opinion was sweeping her along. Everyone now openly talked of her marriage and when she denied it, and got rather heated when doing so, everyone looked sceptical and asked her why she was stalling.

'Only a fool would refuse Dennis,' Janice said bluntly.

Creena's mother looked worried the day

164

Creena said violently that if Dennis was the last man in the world, she would not marry him. 'But Creena dear, are you being fair to him? You have let him believe . . .'

'I have not,' Creena said crossly. 'He just took it for granted and he won't give me a chance to tell him the truth.'

Her mother looked sad. 'That seems rather far-fetched, darling, when you spend all your spare time with him.'

Creena turned away. It was hopeless. She must find some way of getting Dennis to herself and making him listen to her.

Norma followed her into the bedroom; a short plump girl with white powder carefully dabbed over the hated spots on her chin. 'You can't mean that, Creena,' she said unhappily. 'You can't mean to hurt Dennis like that.'

'Look, Norma,' Creena said angrily. 'I'd hurt Dennis a great deal more if I married him without loving him.'

'But why encourage him?' Norma asked.

Creena looked at the ceiling and prayed for patience. 'Look—I'm trying to tell him and he won't give me a chance.'

'Why not write a letter?' Norma flounced to the door. 'I think you're just playing with him. It's beastly of you, Creena.'

Creena thought. 'A *Dear-John* letter,' she said slowly. 'It is very tempting but I've always thought it a cruel cowardly way out.'

'What you are doing now is just as cruel and

165

cowardly,' Norma said and slammed the door.

Norma was right. It was just as cowardly, cruel and childish to go on like this. She went out of the house, walked to where she had parked her small car and drove down to the town to a call box. It was hopeless trying to telephone from home for there was always someone about.

She drove down the wide street, avoiding two dogs who were having a fight in the road, driving carefully round an African woman who was cycling along happily, a baby strapped to her back and a suitcase balanced on her head. The deep yellow of the dress the African woman was wearing was a marvellous contrast to the crimson shawl that strapped the baby and she was cycling steadily along as if there was nothing on her head at all.

Creena parked outside the call box. Inside, she dialled the hospital—Dennis had gone, she was told. Next she dialled the Crampton house. Dennis was in.

'Hi—honey—lovely to hear your voice . . .'

Dennis's voice came clearly but she thought there was an artificial note in it.

'Dennis I must see you . . .' she said desperately. 'Look, I simply must tell you that I can't . . .'

There was a little click and she knew he had replaced the receiver. She found more money and dialled again. She got an engaged sign and she knew that Dennis was deliberately making it impossible for her to reach him.

She drove home, trembling with anger. Maybe Norma was right and when a man won't listen, the only way is to write. After dinner that night, she went to her room and carefully wrote and told Dennis the truth. She posted the letter on her way to work next day.

She was typing a letter when Bart appeared. He was looking strained and worried. 'Creena,' he said, 'could you help me?'

She was startled. It was the first time he had ever asked her for anything.

'Of course,' she said warmly, looking at his unhappy face.

He put a telegram on her desk. 'I've just heard from my mother. She's coming on the bus from Breyten. I can't meet her because I'm operating.'

Creena read the terse message that simply said she was arriving on the bus. Two words were added and they looked like a threat.

'For good.'

She looked up into the anxious face above her. 'Didn't you expect her?'

He frowned. 'Of course not. I'm only here as a locum. I can't understand. We had a flat there—what has she done with it . . . and the furniture . . .' He ran his hand through his hair wearily. 'Oh, dear Creena—she's going to hate it here. It'll be much too quiet for her and . . .' He sighed again.

Creena thought swiftly. 'Look,' she said, her

voice calm and, she hoped, reassuring. 'Suppose I meet the bus and take her home to mother? You won't want her up here and I can't just dump her at the cottage. Then you could come to dinner tonight and pick her up. Could you make arrangements for a bed to go into the cottage or . . .' She saw the worried expression on his face and hastily added: 'Look, Bart, leave it to me. I'll organize everything and you needn't worry about a thing. Just come up to us tonight. I'll explain to your mother that you have a very busy day . . .'

'Thanks—Creena,' was all he said but for a moment his hand closed over hers. She shivered. Then he smiled. 'I'll leave it all to you,' he said gently.

She watched him walk away and she drew a long deep breath. At long last she was going to be allowed to do something to help that man!

CHAPTER TWELVE

Four hectic hours later, Creena was waiting in her car at the bus stop. She had telephoned her mother and explained the situation so that there would be a light cold lunch awaiting Mrs. Darling; in her lunch hour, Creena had gone to Bart's cottage and been rather horrified at its bleakness. A hasty dash round with a duster, going into the hospital grounds for an

168

armful of flowers with which to fill the vases—deep red roses, pink stocks, scented white pinks, blue larkspur—anything to give the bleak little house some colour. Then the bed she had borrowed from the hospital arrived and she made it up in the spare bedroom that was very sparsely furnished with a chest of drawers and small wardrobe. She had ordered groceries and meat and stocked the small refrigerator. She had tried to think of everything so that Bart's mother should not feel unwelcome when she arrived.

And now here she was—watching the cloud of dust in the distance which meant the bus was wending its way down the last steep mountainside and knowing that in a few moments, she would be meeting Bart's mother.

Of course it was absurd, but it seemed to Creena—standing there in her pale blue cotton frock, her red-gold hair rumpled by the breeze, her eyes wide with curiosity—that this was a very important occasion. Somehow she must make Mrs. Darling like her. Somehow . . .

There were crowds of Africans pouring out of the long single-decker bus when it stopped in front of Creena but only two Europeans from the front half of the bus. One was a tall thin man Creena had never seen before, the next—a short slender middle-aged woman in a neat grey suit, a small hat to match with a circlet of violets, a large black shiny handbag clutched tightly in her hands. A frail-looking, meek little woman who gazed round her anxiously, holding the bag close to her as if she was afraid someone might snatch it. The driver was dumping several suitcases on the ground round her but the woman went on looking anxiously for someone she knew.

Somehow it didn't look like Bart's mother. Creena had pictured a much older woman; perhaps a big-boned woman with an authoritative air—not this small timid-looking creature. However she was only the possible . . .

Creena stepped forward. 'Mrs. Darling?' she said gently.

The small woman spun round as if a shot had been fired. Her eyes were a faded blue and were big with fright.

'My boy,' she gasped. 'Something has happened? He is—'

Creena moved closer. 'He is all right, Mrs. Darling. He sends you his love and is terribly sorry but it is his day for operating . . .'

The small woman's spare hand went to her heart. 'Oh, dear me, for a moment you gave me such a fright. I was so afraid . . .' A faint smile flickered over her pale face. 'I should have known. A doctor's mother has to expect to take second-place . . .'

'He would have met you if he could,' Creena assured her. 'I told him I would be happy to meet you. My mother is expecting you for lunch and Bart is fetching you tonight

. . .'

'How very kind of you and your mother,' Mrs. Darling said warmly. She allowed herself to be settled in Creena's small car, watched the luggage tucked in the boot by an African in a bright red shirt and torn khaki shorts. 'One— two . . . oh, dear me there is the third! I have to keep counting them, dear, to make sure they don't get stolen,' she said as Creena slid behind the steering wheel.

Creena smiled reassuringly. 'We don't have things stolen up here. I am Creena Hall,' she said, remembering she ought to introduce herself. 'I work at the hospital—sort of general dog's-body,' she went on with a laugh. 'Secretary and receptionist and—'

Mrs. Darling was peering at her through narrowed eyes. 'Oh, I've heard of you. You're the girl that nice Dr. Tyson is going to marry. My boy has mentioned you in his letters . . .'

Creena was driving down the main street. 'I'm not . . .' she began but Mrs. Darling was not listening. She was twisting her white gloves nervously in her hands, leaning towards Creena, saying plaintively:

'I'm sure you're a good girl—you would tell me the truth? I mean, you often have to be cruel to be kind, don't you? How is Bartie?'

It took Creena a few seconds to grasp that Mrs. Darling was talking of Bart! *Bartie.* It had a nauseating sound. Who could ever call a big impressive man like Bart by such a name?

171

'He is very well,' Creena said, finding it hard to keep her voice even.

Mrs. Darling clutched her arm and, not being prepared for it, Creena let the car lurch and had to hastily straighten it. Mrs. Darling's face was frightened.

'You won't tell me . . . you're lying to me. He's been killed . . .' her voice rose and Creena realized that Bart's mother was almost hysterical.

Creena pulled the car up on the grass verge. Behind them was the town—they were in a narrow tree-lined road, just starting to climb the mountainside. It was very peaceful and hot. She caught hold of Mrs. Darling's hands and held them tightly. 'I swear to you that Bart is all right,' she said loudly. 'I spoke to him half an hour ago on the 'phone. He is fine—and sends his love.'

She felt the tenseness slowly leave Mrs. Darling's arms, felt her slowly relax and then Creena let her go. 'Why were you so frightened?' she asked gently.

'I don't know,' Mrs. Darling looked like a frightened trapped animal. Her hand was at her throat as if she found it hard to breathe. 'I'm so afraid for him. He never thinks—he is so impulsive—does such foolish things.'

It was difficult to believe such statements. Bart—impulsive? Bart—doing foolish things?

'What sort of foolish things?' Creena asked gently.

Mrs. Darling waved her hands vaguely. 'Getting involved with women . . .'

'Bart?' Creena could not help laughing. 'But he's almost a woman-hater. He says a doctor should not marry . . .'

'And he's so right,' Mrs. Darling said fervently, two ugly patches of red showing in her pale cheeks. 'I married a doctor and I know . . .' Her hand flew to her mouth in dismay. 'Oh, dear me, I didn't mean to frighten you. I mean, you are going to marry a doctor and—'

'I am . . .' Creena began indignantly and then sighed. What was the good? Mrs. Darling was not listening. She was opening her handbag, burrowing into its untidy contents.

'Ever since that letter came, I have been afraid. That's why I packed everything and came up here. Bartie must see that I'm right . . . the only thing to do is to go back to England . . .' Mrs. Darling said, her voice shaking.

'Letter?' Creena said.

Mrs. Darling looked up. 'Oh, dear, I don't seem to have it with me. I meant to show it to Bartie. I must have thrown it away by accident. Oh, dear I meant to keep it . . .' Her hands were trembling.

'What was in the letter, Mrs. Darling?'

Mrs. Darling looked up, her eyes filled with tears. 'Oh, it was a terrible letter. It was anonymous and typed and . . . and it said that

173

Bartie was involved with several women here and going to get dismissed and . . . and that if I valued his future I should come and help him . . . so I came,' she finished simply and looked trustingly at Creena. 'Have you heard the gossip? Is he in trouble? Is he getting dismissed?'

Creena found herself shaking with anger. 'Oh, I don't know who wrote that letter . . .' she began angrily.

Mrs. Darling's hand rested on her arm. The fingers tightened round Creena's flesh painfully. 'Tell me the truth,' she said harshly, her eyes bright with suspicion. 'You see, it's happened before. There was a girl—a terrible girl. Laura was her name. There was scandal—I thought they would throw Bartie out . . . might have him struck off the rolls. I was afraid for him . . . that's why when the telegram came I answered it for him.'

Creena felt confused. 'What telegram?'

Mrs. Darling relaxed limply, dropping Creena's arm. 'The telegram from Dr. Tyson. I had met him, you see. He was on holiday and came to East London—he met Bartie at a medical conference, Bartie brought him home. A fine handsome young man. So . . . when the telegram came with his name on it, I knew everything would be all right. He wanted Bartie to take his place because he had been hurt in an accident. I saw this as an escape from the town for Bartie. If he got away maybe

174

the scandal would be forgotten and Laura stop the terrible thing she was doing . . . so I wired back that Bartie would come and—'

'He didn't know anything about it?' Creena tried to imagine Bart's reaction when he got home. He must have been furious.

'Oh, no, not until it was too late to do anything about it.' Mrs. Darling smiled triumphantly. 'That's the way to handle Bartie—never ask him but always do it first and then even if he is annoyed, he is very good at hiding it . . . Anyhow he managed to find someone to take his place and came up here and I could breathe again. I thought he was safe—that here there would be no predatory women—but then the letter came and I was afraid.' Her hand clutched Creena's again. 'You must tell me the truth.'

Creena drew a long deep breath. It was absolutely fantastic. This little faded quiet woman talking like this about Bart? And Bart being involved in some sordid affair with a woman called Laura. Creena refused to believe it. Bart was too careful—too afraid of getting involved with a woman to allow such a thing to happen. But this anonymous letter . . . who could have sent it?

She tried to make her voice firm and reassuring. 'Please, Mrs. Darling, I am telling you the truth. Bart is very well and is most definitely not involved with any woman. There is no scandal about him and they are certainly

175

not dismissing him. He came as a locum as you know but until they are able to replace him with a permanent doctor, Bart will be needed here.'

The small woman stared at the pretty girl for a long time and then seemed to collapse. 'Oh, thank you, dear, that is a weight off my mind. But who wrote to me?'

'I don't know,' Creena said crossly. 'I think it must be some kind of practical joke.'

'But who would . . . and I've rushed up here,' Mrs. Darling wailed. 'How cruel—how terribly terribly cruel. Oh, dear, what shall I do . . .' She rocked herself backwards and forwards as if in pain. 'And I had planned everything so nicely. I would rescue Bartie from the clutches of these women and take him back to England and we would both be so happy . . .'

'Perhaps it will all work out for the best, Mrs. Darling,' Creena said gently. 'You're here now and close to your son. Perhaps when Bart leaves here, he'll take you back to England . . .'

Mrs. Darling clasped her hands tightly. 'Oh, that would be wonderful—too too wonderful. I hate this country . . .' She shuddered.

Creena glanced at her watch. She ought to be back at the hospital by now and her mother would be wondering what had happened to them. She started the car and began to drive. They were crossing the narrow bridge over the dry little river when she thought of something.

'Mrs. Darling,' she said nervously, not sure how to put it into words. 'This is a small community and there is always a lot of . . . of talk so if I were you, I wouldn't talk too much about . . . about Laura and—'

Mrs. Darling sat bolt upright. 'Bartie did nothing disgraceful,' she said stiffly.

Creena's cheeks burned. 'I am sure he didn't—but in a place like this, people twist things and . . . and maybe you shouldn't talk about that anonymous letter you had . . .'

'I have nothing to be ashamed of,' Mrs. Darling's voice was icy. 'It is the writer who should be ashamed.'

'I know but . . .' Creena was driving the car in over the cattle trap and knew it was hopeless. As she stopped, she gazed at the small, meek-looking woman and her heart seemed to miss a beat. What a terrible lot of harm Mrs. Darling could do Bart. Was there no way to stop her?

Half an hour later, having introduced Mrs. Darling to her parents, Creena drove rapidly to the hospital. In the short time she had known her, Mrs. Darling had moaned incessantly on the problems of being a doctor's mother and how selfish all doctors were and how vulnerable and how easily the wrong woman could ruin them. If any woman could ruin Bart, Creena decided, it was his own mother.

Much later that afternoon, Bartie dropped

177

into the little office. It was a slack period, there were visitors in the wards, the doctors were seeing their private patients. Bart had none that day for he never saw private patients on operating day. He looked thoroughly exhausted and worried as he dropped into the chair, stretching out his long legs, running his hands worriedly through his hair.

'How is my mother?' he asked abruptly.

Creena hesitated. She doodled with a pencil on a bit of paper. Should she tell him everything? All her fears? About the anonymous letter and the bit about Laura? But maybe that would look as if she had questioned his mother—as if she was spying on him. He went on without waiting for an answer.

'I suppose she told you that she was used to taking second place? That a woman with a doctor for a son got used to being put on one side?' His voice was bitter and he nodded as he saw by her face that he was right. 'She will never forgive me for following in my father's footsteps.'

'She loves you very much,' Creena ventured. 'She is worried about you.'

Bart moved his big shoulders restlessly. 'She always has been worried about me. She would like to run my life. Sometimes she does . . .' His mouth tightened. 'If only I wasn't so darned sorry for her, Creena,' he said almost desperately. 'She has a distorted mind. She believes that she does these outrageous things for my own good . . .'

'She told me she took this job without you knowing anything about it,' Creena said quietly.

He looked at her. 'How you must despise me,' he said slowly. 'Yes—she wired back acceptance and when I came home that night for dinner, calmly told me about it. I could have refused—could have wired Tyson to say it was impossible but . . . Well, I knew he needed someone pretty urgently to have wired for me—we didn't get on well, I'm afraid,' Bart went on grimly. 'And I didn't want to make my mother look small so I agreed. But what future have I here? The instant they can replace me, they will.'

Creena rested her pointed chin on her hands, her green eyes worried.

'She hopes you'll take her back to England.'

Bart gave a little groan and ran his hand through his hair. 'She never lets me forget that she gave up her beloved England for me . . .' He looked at Creena. 'Maybe you think I'm soft. After all, I am an adult . . .' He smiled wryly, 'But I am sorry for her. I even have a sort of guilt complex about her because doctors—my father and I—have made her so lonely and unhappy. I'd give anything to make her happy but I can't do that at the cost of my work. I told you she lived with her sister at one time and they fought wildly—if I walked out

179

on her, she would only have that sister to fall back on for comfort . . . I know she means well but . . .'

Creena was searching for the right words. 'I wish . . . I wish . . . oh, Bart, I'm worried about your mother. She . . . she talks so much. I'm terrified she'll talk like that to someone like Mrs. Isipin and . . .' She paused, startled by his angry look, wishing she had kept her mouth shut.

'About what?' he asked curtly.

Creena swallowed. 'About—Laura.'

There was silence. Then Bart stood up, his eyes sparking fire. 'Mother has been talking, I see,' he said grimly. 'Well, believe me or not, Creena, there was nothing—but nothing— between Laura and me. It was a misunderstanding. A neurotic . . .' He paused, swallowing hard as if trying not to say things he might regret. And then he turned and walked out of the office.

Alone she finished her typing, covered the typewriter and was picking up her things when she realized she had hardly seen Dennis all that day. There had been so much excitement—so much to do . . . She glanced at her watch. He would have finished seeing his private patients by now.

She walked down the corridor and met him coming out of his surgery. He hesitated in the doorway and then came to meet her. He smiled.

'Everything settled—the old lady finally delivered?'

Puzzled, she asked him what he meant.

'Why Mrs. Darling, of course. You were meeting her, I'm told.'

'Yes. She's at home, Bart is fetching her tonight . . .'

'Very kind of you.' Dennis said cheerfully, walking by her side. 'What do you think of the old girl? Round the bend, I'd say. I met her, you know.'

'She told me.'

Dennis looked down at her. 'What are you mad about, honey? Me?'

'I'm not mad, just . . .' Creena hesitated. Dennis disliked Bart—he would be no friend of his. He was the last person she must talk to about Mrs. Darling. And then she remembered. She looked up at him. 'Did you get my letter, Dennis?'

A strange look flicked across his face. 'Letter?' he said. 'What letter?'

'I wrote to you. You should have got it in this afternoon's mail.'

'Oh.' He smiled at her, cupped her bare elbow with his hand and squeezed it. 'I haven't opened my mail yet. I'll answer it when I've read it.' He smiled down into her eyes. 'Must run, honey, be seeing you . . .' he said, and was off down the corridor striding fast.

She watched him go. And knew that he had lied to her. He had read her letter—but he had

181

no intention of accepting her decision. What was her next move? She could hardly insert an announcement in the local paper to say she was not going to marry Dr. Tyson, could she?

CHAPTER THIRTEEN

Later that evening, after a dinner which had seemed interminable, with Mrs. Darling constantly talking about the trials of a doctor's mother and how she missed her dear England, Creena and Bart went outside for a stroll. His mother was happily playing bridge with Dr. and Mrs. Hall and a neighbour who had come over for a game; Mike was out somewhere and Norma had retired to her bedroom to do her prep.

It was a perfect night. Warm, not the slightest ripple of a breeze to disturb the trees. Every now and then, one of Mrs. Hall's fowls would flutter their wings or make a little squeaking noise. Once a horse neighed.

Creena and Bart strolled across the well-cut grass to the swing chair, the three dogs close to their sides. Samson was next to Bart, looking up with bright expectant eyes, Quido, the black Labrador had Creena's hand in his soft mouth as they strolled along and Rudi was running ahead excitedly, wriggling his slim shiny body.

Sitting on the swing chair, they gazed across

the moon-lit valley to the dark mountains beyond. Creena relaxed. How beautiful—how still. The scent of the ghost-like white tobacco plants teased their noses. How romantic . . .

'Thanks for making my cottage look so inviting,' Bart said abruptly. 'I had quite a shock when I went home to change. You've certainly made it look nice. You must have gone to a lot of trouble.'

Creen smiled. 'I enjoyed it. I wanted your mother to feel welcome.'

Bart looked unhappy. 'It's very good of you but . . .'

He sighed. 'You heard how she feels. Nothing short of taking her back to England will make her happy.'

'I don't know how you stand it,' Creena said impulsively. 'I mean, when she came out here, she must have known it would be different. After all, it is your work. Doesn't it depress you? The way she moans, I mean.' Her face was suddenly red. 'Oh, that sounds awfully rude I didn't mean to—'

He chuckled. 'I know what you mean, Creena. Yes, it does get me down at times but usually I'm so tired, I just don't listen. It relieves her feelings, I suppose, so it's doing some good.' He smiled at her. 'All the same, Creena'—he said her name so deliberately that it was like a caress—'thanks for making the cottage look so attractive.'

'It was a pleasure.' Somehow being so alone

183

in the moon-lit black night with the shadows creeping up to enclose them, she felt gay, carefree, unafraid of what he might think. 'Quite a pleasant change,' she went on teasingly, 'to be able to do something for the self-sufficient Dr. Darling.'

Bart turned sideways to look at her. He laughed. 'Do I appear to be so self-sufficient?'

'Oh, yes, indeed you do,' Creena laughed back. 'The perfect bachelor—needing no one.'

He frowned momentarily. 'I'm not really self-sufficient, you know. Tell me, Creena.' His voice had changed, now it was amused as if he was laughing at her. 'Can you tell me why all girls have this maternal urge? You're like all the rest. I've not met a girl yet who didn't want to tell me to get my hair cut or offer to darn my socks. When I was at medical school, I hadn't enough socks to go round for all the girls who wanted to mend them. What is this urge to fuss over men—why?'

Creena's cheeks were hot. *Touché,* she thought. Her first impression on seeing Bart had been that he needed a haircut! Her second was that she wondered who sewed on missing buttons and darned his socks.

'Don't you know . . .' she said, her voice brittle with brightness. 'It's what Sinatra sang about—"the Tender Trap." Didn't you see the film? it was very good.'

'"The Tender Trap"? Yes, I remember now, I did see it. So you would say that all

184

maternally-minded girls are setting a trap?' He was still laughing at her.

'Not consciously, perhaps,' she said gravely. 'Remember you told me once how very different it was for a man to think of love. Love to him meant responsibilities, a curtailment of his liberty, perhaps a frustration of his ambitions. That every girl looked forward to marriage. I think you're right and I think when we have this desire to do something for a man, like mend his socks or bake him a cake, it is probably a subconscious desire to prove to him that we would make good wives.'

'You're sure it is a subconscious desire?' he teased.

Creena had found her gaiety had vanished. She was suddenly filled with the need to know more about this man. 'Why haven't you ever married, Bart? Was your heart broken or something?'

As if in key with her change of character, he sobered and answered with equal gravity. 'No—certainly not. It is as I told you. I saw the unhappy difficult life my father led and I decided that doctors are happier single. So are the girls they might have married. It is no life for a woman . . .'

'Mother didn't mind. I . . .'

Bart looked at her oddly. 'Your mother is an unusual woman and she happens to love your father very much. She is a mature person and

185

probably was like that as a girl.'

'Am I mature?' Creena asked. It was a silly question and she regretted it the next moment, but Bart didn't seem to think so.

'Yes—I would say you are very mature for your age.'

'I . . . I'd . . . make a good doctor's wife.'

With an abrupt movement Bart was on his feet. 'I'm sure you will,' he said curtly. 'I only hope Tyson appreciates his good fortune.'

Creena stood up quickly, her hand on his sleeve. 'Bart—Dennis and I—'

Before she could say any more they heard a voice. 'Bartie—'

'Mother,' Bart said.

They were standing side by side, Creena still with her hand on his arm as she looked up into his face. 'Bart, please . . .' she said urgently.

Maybe if the moon hadn't chosen that moment to hide behind a cloud—maybe if Creena hadn't moved a little and stumbled against him—maybe then Bart wouldn't have taken her in his arms.

It seemed an endless moment as she put her arms round his neck and held him close, her mouth warm and responsive under his . . . She had read once that when you kiss the man you love, it is as if all the music in the world was playing, the sun shining, the birds singing. The book was right. It was just like that. Time stood still while you were, for a moment, in Paradise.

186

'Bartie—Bartie . . .' The voice was sharper, imperative.

Slowly, reluctantly, Bart released Creena. He gazed down at her thoughtfully. 'I'm sorry,' he said jerkily. 'I had no right . . .' He turned away. Creena close behind.

'Don't be sorry—Bart,' she said urgently. 'I'm not. Bart, Dennis and I aren't—'

'Coming, Mother,' Bart called, just as if Creena had not spoken.

She stood still, shivering a little. Had she frightened him, revealed her love too plainly?

Somehow she made herself follow the tall broad-shouldered man, somehow she said good-bye to Mrs. Darling, somehow she acted as if nothing had happened but inside her there was a cold desolation. Had she embarrassed Bart?

Before she went to bed, Creena found herself alone with her father for a moment. He looked at her, his face troubled.

'I wish Mrs. Darling hadn't come here,' he said slowly. 'I'm afraid for Bart. A doctor is so vulnerable, Creena, and gossip is so rife in this place. What is all this about a girl called Laura?'

Creena shrugged. 'I don't know, Dad. I asked Bart and he was furious. Asked me if his mother had been talking—he said Laura was just neurotic.'

'Probably some predatory female trying to dig her claws in him,' Dr. Hall said curtly.

187

'Trouble is as a doctor you can so easily run into trouble. A sex-mad girl imagines things that don't happen but her talk could ruin even the best of men. His mother seems to think the girl could have caused a great deal of trouble. A very hysterical type,' he added disapprovingly. 'She doesn't love Bart—she just loves Mrs. Darling.' He paused. 'I'm afraid she's the answer to Mrs. Isipin's prayer.'

Creena was to remember those words in the weeks ahead. It was quite shocking the way the gossip flew through the little town. Everyone was talking about Bart Darling and about his mother's extraordinary remarks; everyone was asking who Laura was and making wild guesses as to what Dr. Darling could have done to make his mother so worried and upset. Slowly, almost intangibly, local thought veered round and now it was Dennis who was approved of and Bart about whom people began to talk warily. What did they know about him? What sort of background had he? If his mother was so alarmed it must be pretty serious . . . you couldn't have smoke without fire . . .

Creena heard all these things and vehemently denied them. Her father was doing the same. Mike was involved in several fights at school but Norma merely said she had never thought much of Bart!

Dennis was behaving strangely, too. He was always so cheerful. He would make a great fuss of Creena in public—would arrange to pick her up that evening, always talking about it in the hall of the hospital and yet, shortly after she got home, a telephone call would come through pleading an emergency, or a change of plan because Mrs. Crampton wanted him to do something for her. It didn't make sense but it suited Creena very well. Since the embarrassing scene with Bart, she had felt that her so-called engagement to Dennis was a shield, Bart could not really think . . .

Meg came to her one day. 'Creena, have you heard the latest?' she demanded, her face red.

'No?' Creena glanced anxiously down the corridor. Voices carried so plainly from the hall yet no one seemed to realize it.

Meg bent forward and lowered her voice. 'I hear Mrs. Darling got an anonymous letter about . . . about Dr. Darling and that's why she came here. She is trying to find out the names of the women with whom he is supposed to be involved.'

Creena sighed. 'Look, Meg, it would be easier to find a needle in a hay-stack than to find any women Bart could be involved with—he just stays away from women.'

'I know,' Meg said ruefully. Her face reddened. 'But Mrs. Darling got hold of my name and tore strips off me.'

'She did?' Creena gasped. 'She has no right.'

'She says she has every right to protect her

189

own child. Creena . . . she sees him as a child . . . too young to care for himself. It's crazy. There isn't a man in the world so capable of looking after himself as Bart Darling,' she added, her voice bitter.

Creena found herself in sympathy. 'You're telling me,' she said with feeling. 'If all men were like Bart, the world would come to an end.'

'Why is he so . . . so women-allergic?' Meg asked with a giggle.

'I don't think he hates women,' Creena said carefully. 'It's just that he doesn't think a doctor should marry. He says it's not fair to the woman.'

'Surely that's her look-out?'

'That's what I said . . .'

'It's all right for you . . .' Meg said enviously. 'Dennis will never be the conscientious kind.'

It was suddenly too much for Creena. It was the proverbial last straw. Only that morning her mother had got excited about some white lace that had been on sale in the store. Just the thing for a wedding-dress, she had said—and Mrs. Crampton on her way through the hospital had paused by the little office and smiled coyly at Creena and asked her if she wasn't taking rather a long time to make up her mind. Creena had been about to tell her the truth but, as usual, something had interrupted her. Now she looked at her watch. She must do it at once, before she changed her mind.

'I want to speak to Dennis. His surgery should be over—I may catch him . . .' she said breathlessly and almost ran down the corridor to the surgeries. Dennis was in the doorway of one, saying good-bye to his last patient. Creena, prepared for opposition or delaying tactics, swept forward, almost forcing him back into his surgery, closing the door behind her and leaning against it. This time she would make him listen and understand.

'Dennis—you must listen this time,' she said violently. 'I cannot marry you. I don't love you and—'

Dennis faced her squarely. He was leaning against his desk, his arms folded. There was an odd look on his face. 'I am sorry,' he said coolly.

She was taken aback. Nothing had prepared her for this cool acceptance. She had expected anything but this. A violent quarrel perhaps. A refusal to listen to her . . . But this quiet subdued man staring at her, his face sad . . . this was something new. He was silent and it seemed an endless time as they simply stared at one another. In the end, the awfulness of the silence forced her to speak.

'I am sorry, Dennis but . . . but it wouldn't be fair to—'

He turned away. 'Wouldn't be fair to you,' he said almost wearily. 'I know. I'm just—very sorry.'

She stood still, twisting her hands nervously. Oh, why had he to take it like this? Surely he must have sensed—must have known all along that she did not love him.

He turned and for a moment she caught her breath. All expression seemed to have been wiped off his face. She had never seen Dennis look defeated before.

'That's all right, Creena,' he said awkwardly. 'No hard feelings. If you don't love me you don't and that's all there is to it . . .' He looked down at the desk and doodled on it with his forefinger. 'I was just wondering if . . .' He hesitated. 'If you would do me a favour?' He looked up at her quickly. 'It would only be for a few months . . .' he added hastily. 'You see . . .'

He walked about the room nervously as he spoke while Creena stayed where she was, leaning against the door.

'You see, Creena, it means so much to me. Mrs. Crampton being fond of me, I mean. I've always been so lonely. An orphan feels sort of adrift in the world, if you know what I mean.' He stared out of the window for a moment. Over his shoulder she could see the mountains rising against the blue sky, the white of the hospital walls, the glint of the windows with the sunshine on them, could hear the laughter and chatter of the African patients. 'Mrs. Crampton is leaving me the hospital in her will—I told you that. She is talking of putting me in sole charge . . . she says I need you, Creena.' His voice was strangely lifeless, dull. 'She's right. I need someone like you—decent, kind. Someone to make me sober up and realize my responsibilities.' He turned to face her. 'If she knows you've thrown me over, she'll probably change her will, Creena. Could you . . . would you . . . would you pretend for three months that we are going to be married? Give me a chance to prove to her that I am reliable . . .'

It hurt her to have him pleading with her . . . it was so unlike Dennis. It even frightened her a little. But she knew that she did not want to agree—she did not want everyone to think she was going to marry Dennis. Not even for three months.

'Dennis, I—'

He gave her no time. 'Creena, please listen to me. Darling has already wormed himself into Mrs. Crampton's good books. He is after the hospital, I'm sure. He is telling her that he is an expert on tropical diseases, that he could get the hospital well-known because of that . . . you see, Creena, it isn't fair. I have to stand on my own feet. Darling has a wealthy mother. She must have money . . . plenty of it.' He came closer and caught hold of her hands, looking down at her earnestly. 'Creena—it means so much to me. My whole future. I have wonderful plans. Once I am in charge it will be a different hospital. We'll enlarge, have that blood bank we need so badly a bigger operating theatre—I'll enlarge the African wards, be able to accept more T.B. patients . . .' his voice was eager and excited.

She tugged at her hands to free them but his clasp tightened.

'Creena . . .' he begged. 'Please . . . don't rush it. Just think about it. Three months and then we'll part. You'll have helped me so much . . . Just think . . . It is not much to ask—we've been friends for a long time . . . Just think . . .'

He let her go and went to stand by the window, gazing out. In the silence she stared at his back. He sounded so sincere, so desperate. Was it too much to ask of her.

Dennis spoke abruptly. 'Did you see the girl when she came in?'

'What girl?'

He swung round, a surprised look on his face. 'Darling's Laura, of course. She arrived on the bus. Didn't you hear about it? The whole town is talking. Went straight into his arms.' Dennis chuckled. 'I gather she's quite something.'

A chill depression gripped Creena. 'Did you see her?'

Dennis shook his head. 'Nary a sign but then he wouldn't bring her up here and run the risk of her meeting his mother. He took her out to one of the new hotels, I was told. I don't know which one. I gather she was quite a dish. Looks as if he had better taste than I gave him credit for . . .'

Laura—here. The woman his mother feared? The woman who could ruin Bart's life? Yet he had welcomed her warmly, smuggled her away somewhere. It didn't make sense. Then he was already committed. Was that why he had apologized for kissing her. Why it suited him to believe she was going to marry Dennis?

And then she had another thought. How plainly she had shown him that she loved him. How warmly she had kissed him. Her cheeks burned as she remembered the way she had clung to him, her arms tightly round his neck. How embarrassed and fearful he must have been of her. He had such a poor opinion of women as it was. And his teasing—his remarks about the way girls fussed over him. Maybe he had not been teasing—maybe it was his way of warning her off . . .

She drew a long shuddering breath. 'All right, Dennis,' she said with difficulty. 'I'll be engaged to you for three months . . .' Anything was better than to let Bart think she loved him. Dennis would be her shield.

Dennis moved swiftly. 'You are an angel,' he said warmly. In a moment, he was sliding a diamond ring on her finger, lifting her hand to his mouth and kissing it lightly. 'I can never thank you enough,' he said. 'You'll never regret this, Creena. I promise not to be a nuisance.'

She managed a smile. Now she was committed—but it was only for three months.

Somehow she drove home. She was too confused and tired to ask how but her mother had heard the news. Dennis must be spreading it round the hospital and town as fast as he could. Oh, well, it did not matter. Nothing mattered now.

'Darling,' her mother was saying, 'now we can start planning the wedding.'

'We'll be engaged six months at least,' Creena said firmly.

'Oh, Creena, it's not fair,' Norma chimed in angrily. 'You keep poor Dennis dangling on a piece of string . . .'

Later her father took her aside. 'Creena— are you sure you are doing the right thing?'

She was tempted to tell him the truth. And then thought that he might tell Bart—and Bart was the last person who must know the truth. Now! Or he might let the truth slip out and that would not be fair to Dennis. She must keep the promise she had made. 'Quite sure, Dad,' she said firmly.

The telephone bell shrilled. It was for her. She heard Mrs. Darling's agitated voice on the line. 'Creena, Creena . . . tell me the truth. I can trust you. Is it true that Laura has come here? That she is with Bartie?'

A terrible lassitude filled Creena. The news was already all over the town. 'I suppose it is the truth,' she said wearily. 'I've not seen her myself but . . . but I hear she came on the bus today.'

'Oh, dear, my poor Bartie . . . my poor Bartie . . .' she heard Mrs. Darling saying anxiously and she replaced the receiver.

CHAPTER FOURTEEN

Life became, for Creena, something of a nightmare. Her mother insisted on throwing an engagement party, everyone kept congratulating her, only Creena's father was very quiet and often she caught him looking at her anxiously.

Dennis, himself, was amazingly helpful, Creena found. In public he was very attentive, just nicely loving, but as soon as they were on their own, he became impersonal, sometimes almost formal.

'You're an angel, Creena,' he said to her several times. 'You keep your side of the bargain and I'll keep mine.'

That was one of the reasons she could not tell her father the truth and so set his mind at rest. Also why, when Bart sought her out and looked gravely down into her eyes and asked her if she was sure she was doing the right thing, she had to find the courage to stare back at him unblinkingly and to assure him that she knew what she was doing. Something very like a stab of pain shot through her as she looked at him. How much had her responsive kiss betrayed? And then she remembered Laura!

She still had not seen Laura. Apparently she was staying at one of the many hotels scattered round the beautiful countryside. Neither had Mrs. Darling, who was daily growing more and more agitated.

'Creena . . .' Meg burst into the little office one day, her face red with anger. 'Have you heard the latest?'

Creena stopped typing and looked up. Meg, the serene. Meg, so calm and cool and collected was just a bundle of nerves these days.

'Someone, Creena . . .' she began dramatically—or as dramatically as she could in a whisper! 'Someone is trying to run Bart out of town.'

Creena sighed. These days she was always being besieged—either by a hysterical Mrs. Darling or an angry Meg. Bart seemed to have plenty of women eager to fight his battles. 'Look,' she said wearily. 'Bart Darling is a man not a child. No one could run him out of town unless he wanted to run. Why not relax, Meg, and leave it to him. He doesn't like people interfering in his affairs.'

'It's our affair, too,' Meg said indignantly. Her smooth black hair was no longer so well disciplined, wisps escaping from under her white cap. 'We may lose the best doctor this hospital has ever had.' For a moment, she looked confused. 'That's not meant to be rude to Dennis, Creena,' she added hastily. 'He is a surgeon rather than a physician. Bart . . . Look,' she began again, perched on the desk, keeping a wary eye on the corridor. 'We all know that Mrs. Darling received an anonymous letter. Right? Who wrote it? Someone who wanted to make trouble for Bart. Then why did this Laura woman come here? I reckon someone sent for her . . .' She smiled thinly at Creena's shocked look. 'Well—isn't it logical? Why else should the woman turn up just at this moment? By the way, have you seen her?'

'No. Have you?' Creena asked in turn.

Meg shook her head violently. 'I have not—yet, It's . . . it's all so mysterious, Creena. No one knows her surname—not even Mrs. Darling for I asked her. So I can't ring up the hotels to find out where she is staying. Is she very young or old or—'

'Dennis's words were, if I remember rightly,' Creena said stiffly, 'that she was quite something.'

'Mrs. Darling is scared out of her wits,' Meg went on. 'Seems to think Laura could ruin Bart's career. I wonder what—'

'Oh, Meg.' Creena felt she could stand no more of it. 'You know as well as I do that doctors are vulnerable. Why, Dad was telling me that when he was Bart's age, he had a

199

frightful time with hysterical or romantic patients who fell in love with him. He always teases Mummy and says he only married her for protection.'

'That's as may be,' Meg said gravely. 'But Mrs. Darling is too anxious for it to be little. Maybe this girl is going to sue him for breach of promise or . . .' she paused, her face horrified.

Creena took a deep breath. 'Don't be stupid,' she said sharply. 'I know Bart would never do anything wrong. I'm sure he would never break a promise . . .'

Meg's eyes were narrowed suddenly, her voice hostile. 'I know it, too, but things can be twisted.'

'I think they are being twisted here.'

Meg nodded triumphantly. 'Ah—now you're coining round to my way of thinking. That's where we began. Someone is trying to ruin Bart—to drive him away. Who can it be?' She jumped to her feet. 'Must go . . .' She was looking at her watch as she sped down the corridor.

Alone, Creena doodled absent-mindedly on a scrap of paper. Could Meg be right? That anonymous letter—some one must have written it. Who? Why? On an impulse, she turned to the records that were kept about the staff. As she had thought, there was very little information about Bart. That was because she had been ill when he arrived and somehow had never got round to getting the usual information for the records. The important point was—there was no address. So that meant that whoever wrote to Mrs. Darling, must have known Bart's address. That eliminated anyone who could only have had access to the hospital records. But who, in town, knew him?

She shivered suddenly despite the heat. She gazed outside at the cloudless blue sky—the distant mountains piling up, the lush green valley with the small town, the familiar groups of walking African patients in their absurd long white nightshirts and small woollen caps.

No one. No one at all. Only one person, to her knowledge, knew of Bart and that was Dennis. But who had sent the telegram to Bart? Besides it couldn't be Dennis. The anonymous letter was typed.

She began to make some discreet inquiries and learned that Dennis had given Bart's name and address to Dr. Pipp. That his wife had been at the hospital and he had given her the telegram to send. Which meant that Rosalie Pipp . . .

And Dennis had said she hated Bart. No, but that was wrong. For Rosalie couldn't type either. She was always saying how helpless she was, that her parents had never let her learn how to do anything that could make her independent.

Suppose—just suppose—Mrs. Darling had

invented the letter? She had never produced it and it had served as a useful excuse to come up here. Yet was Mrs. Darling really as ruthless as that? Surely no mother could deliberately risk her son's whole future because of a selfish desire to leave the country? Yet Creena knew that, according to her father, mother-love could be queerly distorted at times. Perhaps Mrs. Darling really believed she was helping Bart.

As though in answer to her thoughts, Bart Darling came striding down the corridor to stand, tall and impressive above her, as he gave her a note.

'Could you send a wire for me right away?' he asked politely. She took the note, glancing at it quickly and then looked up.

'I didn't know Mrs. Crampton was ill.'

Bart's mouth was a grim line. 'Nor did anyone else. I had to ring her about someone and she told me she was in bed. Of course Tyson is her doctor and he may not have thought it necessary to tell anyone . . .'

'I would have sent her some flowers,' Creena said. In the past days she and Mrs. Crampton had grown more friendly. Mrs. Crampton was so pleased about the engagement and suddenly Creena had seen her—not as a difficult tyrannical miserly old lady but as a lonely woman, trying to stretch her money, trying to make herself necessary to someone.

'Well—I'll probably get struck off the rolls for this . . . to quote my mother,' Bart said with a wry smile. 'But I'm asking an old friend of mine up here for the week-end. He's a heart specialist and I'm going to get him to have a quiet look at Mrs. Crampton. It is not,' he added hastily as if just remembering that Creena was engaged to Dennis, 'that I am suggesting Tyson doesn't know what he is doing. He is brilliant at snap diagnosis but she is a very frightened woman and I sometimes wonder if Tyson allows for this. I feel that she is troubled unduly about her health, that she dwells on it and so it becomes a vicious circle—she worries in case she will be ill, makes herself ill and then has a reason for being worried and so it goes on.' He laughed without humour. 'Actually she is very annoyed with me. I don't know what I've done but she says there is a lot of gossip about me.' His eyes were suddenly cold as he looked at Creena. 'Perhaps you could enlighten me. What have I done wrong this time?'

Her face hot, she hesitated. 'Surely your mother—'

Bart waved a hand impatiently. 'Let's leave her out. She is always telling me I am being talked about and I never listen. What is it this time?'

Creena took a deep breath. 'Laura.'

'Laura?' His face turned a dull angry red. 'What the—'

203

'Bart—you asked me and . . . if you want the truth, they wonder why Laura has come here.'

'Come here?' He stared at her angrily. 'Are you mad? Mother is always talking about Laura but then she always was. She deliberately . . .' He paused, biting his lips, scowling ferociously. 'Forget it,' he went on curtly. 'Is Laura supposed to be here? Mother asked me but I put it down to one of her bouts of wishful thinking.'

'Wishful thinking?' Creena echoed.

He went red again. 'Forget it. I'm talking too much. Look—is this wretched creature supposed to be here?'

Creena nodded. 'Yes. And you are supposed to have met her at the bus stop, given her a very loving welcome and immediately driven her away to some romantic hideout where you visit her discreetly.' She spoke in a fierce whisper, tired of his moods, tired of—of everything.

Bart leaned against the wall of the little room and folded his arms. She saw that he was laughing silently. 'Well . . . blow me down,' he said in a comical voice. 'The way this town talks. Of course it isn't true. Laura isn't here. Why should she be—she has a perfectly good husband of her own.'

Creena felt suddenly weak. Somehow she had built up a tremendous romance between Bart and the unknown Laura. 'She has?'

'Sure she has. And a fine doctor Crawford

is, too. There was nothing to it, Creena. She was my patient and she was mad with her husband and so fell in love with the person most conveniently near. Happened to be me, her doctor. It happens all the time. Doesn't mean a thing. She wrote me a few letters, 'phoned a few times and my mother built up a big something of it—' He stopped abruptly, passed his hand through his hair agitatedly. 'Oh . . . shucks.' The words sounded odd on his lips but he suddenly looked very young and unsure. 'I don't want to be disloyal to my mother. I'm sure she sincerely believes that she does everything to help me but . . . but if only she would leave me alone. Laura's infatuation died as rapidly as it began and at this moment she and her husband are in England. He's gone over for a refresher course . . .'

'Why don't you tell your mother?'

His mouth tightened. 'I will.'

They were interrupted by Dr. Pipp. The short plump bald man was agitated.

'Oh, Darling, I was looking for you. Have just had a cable from New York that they want me to go over right away. I've had to cancel my bookings and make fresh ones. What I'm worried about is that Mrs. Carter . . . she was badly injured in a car accident. She has a history of some significance . . .' He took Bart by the arm and they turned away, Dr. Pipp's voice urgent. ' . . . drip of Dextrone . . blood

pressure low . . . some peritoneal irritation . . .'
Creena could hear no more as the two men
walked away.

At home, that evening, Creena asked her
father to stroll up to the paddock with her.
'Snow-White seems to have a sore foot, Dad.
Would you look at her?'

'Sure . . .' He stood up at once and smiled at
her. Mrs. Hall was knitting a bright red
pullover. Mike was sprawled all over the
couch, biting a pencil viciously as he scowled at
a book of poems.

'Good—hi, Ma—hear me again, will you?'
he asked in a strangely deep voice.

His mother smiled at him. 'Of course. Toss
me the book.' She caught it easily and looked
at the words. 'Go ahead . . .'

Mike began reciting in a flat wooden voice,
his eyes screwed up as he concentrated.

'Help,' Creena whispered to her father in
mock dismay. 'Thanks be my schooling days
are behind me.'

It was very quiet outside the comfortable
cheerful house. They walked across the dark
grass almost silently, her hand tucked through
his arm. Occasionally a chicken would cluck—
or a bird in a tree move—and a frog croaked
mournfully. The lights in the valley below were
twinkling as if in sympathy with the thousands
of stars that made such a wonderful picture in
the dark bowl of sky. The moon was warmly
golden and lighted a path for them.

Creena began abruptly. 'Snow-White is fine, Dad, I just wanted a chance to talk to you. Today Meg came to me and . . .' Briefly she condensed all that Meg had said and finished: 'She seems to think someone wants to run Bart out of town.'

'Could be,' her father said thoughtfully. 'There certainly is an active campaign going on at the moment about this girl, Laura. Have you seen her?'

'No—and she isn't even here . . .' Creena told him, and repeated all that Bart had told her.

Her father didn't seem surprised. 'Lots of patients are like that. They feel angry with their husbands and a doctor is a convenient handle on which to hang their need to be loved. One has to be careful. I never thought for a moment that Bart Darling was involved in any scandal.'

For some ridiculous reason, she glowed with pleasure. 'You like Bart.'

'I do. I like him as a man, I respect him as a fine doctor. Now, let's get this tangled web straightened out. First, Mrs. Darling has an anonymous letter. Who sent it? Why did they send it? Secondly, someone has invented the story that Laura here, trying to get Bart so involved in scandal that . . .' They had reached the upper road. It was still and dark under the tall wattle trees. Scents from the various flowers drifted towards them, in the paddock the horses were dark shadows. From the compound higher up the mountain, came the sounds of the drums. The drums played all the time, every night, and rarely did Creena notice them. Tonight in the still of the darkness, they sounded loud, almost ominous.

Her father spoke abruptly. 'I think Meg might be right.'

'But who?'

He looked down at her. 'His mother.' He paused while she digested the startling thought, and suddenly it was not so startling after all. It was almost logical. 'You see, Creena,' her father went on slowly. 'Mrs. Darling is actually a deluded woman. Self-deluded. She is a romantic and yearns for someone to need her, to love her only. She is a one-man woman but she wants that one man to live only for her. Only that would prove his love for her, she thinks. Well, her husband failed her. His job came first. With Bart it is the same. She cannot forgive or forget it but now she has transferred her hatred from Bart to his job. She tells herself that if only Bart was not a doctor—he would love her, would spend every moment of his time with her. In other words, everything would he hunky-dory.'

'But she must be mad . . .' Creena burst out. 'You can't—'

'She's lived for so long in a slough of self-pity that she has lost all sense of values. I would also guarantee that she honestly believes that it is for Bart's good.'

'That's what he said,' Creena told her father.

There was a silence. 'You like Bart—quite a lot, don't you?' her father asked quietly.

She was glad the darkness would hide her red cheeks. 'Yes . . . yes, I do,' she admitted and then hurried on: 'But I'm not in love with him, Daddy, if that's what you mean. He warned me at the beginning,' she went on, her voice bitter. 'He is afraid of women because they mean marriage—and to him, that would be destruction.'

'You can understand why,' her father mused as they strolled over the grass, wet from the heavy night dew. 'See what his mother did to his father, what she is trying to do to him, now.'

'Dad!' Mike's shout came clearly through the quiet night. 'Tellee . . . phone!' he shouted, drawlingly.

'Oh, Dad . . .' Creena said as they hurried to the house. 'Who could it be?'

'Might be Dr. Pipp . . .' Her father spoke over his shoulder. 'Rang me earlier. Seems he has to be off at once and he is worried about Mrs. Carter.'

'Mm.' He was telling Bart . . .'

At the doorway, her father paused. 'It isn't that he doesn't trust Bart. It's just that Mrs. Carter has been his patient for many years and he wishes he didn't have to rush off like this and leave her in a stranger's hands.'

Inside the house, Mrs. Hall was at the telephone. 'Yes, Rosalie,' she was saying sympathetically. 'A doctor's wife does not have an easy life . . . Here is my husband . . .' Her eyes were twinkling as she gave the receiver to Dr. Hall. 'Poor Rosalie,' she said softly as she went back to her seat. 'She is very upset because she isn't going with him to America.'

'He'd have more money if she spent less on her back,' Mike said bluntly.

'Mike.' His mother remonstrated lightly. 'All the same, you are right. She is an extravagant little thing but if he doesn't mind . . .'

'I bet he regrets marrying her,' Mike said, sliding down on the couch, stretching his legs in the air. 'A doctor should stay single—he travels fastest who travels alone . . .'

'You're quoting Bart,' Creena said and suddenly she wanted to cry.

Their father quietly replaced the receiver and looked at his lanky long-legged son with a grin. 'Remember, Mike, it can be awfully lonely travelling alone and it isn't everyone who wants to travel fast. Pick your wife wisely and it helps . . . All the same, it isn't an easy life for a wife . . .'

'I don't agree at all,' Mrs. Hall said mildly, her needles clicking. 'After all no one forces you to marry a doctor. You go into it with your eyes open. I mean, no marriage is easy. You always have to adjust yourself. Think of being married to a travelling salesman, away five nights out of every week, always wondering what he was up to . . .' Her eyes twinkled at Mike who was looking somewhat shocked. It was her amused contention that your children expected you to live in a glass house, innocent, ignorant but understanding! In other words, you must always behave like a mother. 'Or being married to a sailor, away for months on end—or a deep-sea diver, risking his life each time . . .'

'Stop—Ma . . .' Creena said laughingly. 'If you talk like that, no girl would ever dare risk getting married.' She escaped to her bedroom and there stood, hugging herself. She wanted to be a doctor's wife . . . but only the wife of a certain doctor. And that was something Bart would never do—marry.

CHAPTER FIFTEEN

It seemed as if nothing could go right that day. Appointments cancelled, fresh ones made; accounts queried; an arrangement made where-by an ambulance came to fetch a patient to take him to Johannesburg; Creena felt rushed off her feet at the hospital but all the time, through the hurly-burly of it ran a thread of fear. What was she going to do? When she and Dennis publicly broke off their engagement, she would have to decide. If Bart stayed on at the hospital indefinitely—and so far, no replacement had been engaged—then Creena knew she would have to go away. It was difficult enough as it was to behave normally but when she no longer had Dennis to hide behind, no longer had Dennis's ring on her finger then, she would have to make a move.

It was absurd to love a man who hardly saw you. Surely she should have more pride? Yet it was the truth. Just to hear his footstep in the corridor—to get a glimpse of his thick fair hair—to hear his voice. If this was love, then she had had no idea it was like this. Agony, frustration . . . was this what Dennis felt for her? That was hard to believe. If he was really heartbroken by her refusal to marry him, he could not behave so casually. Even as she thought this, Dennis was there; handsome with his dark smooth hair, his dark eyes, his charming voice as he bent over the desk, his arm lightly round her shoulders, his voice soft in her ear.

'I'm going to be tied up tonight, Creena, but no one must know. Okay?'

She smiled at him. 'Okay.' It would give her time to do some of those little jobs that keep being postponed. Her nails—trying that new hairdo—answer the letter she had had from Audrey.

Dennis straightened. 'Thanks, honey. I'll

pick you up round about eight o'clock, then?'

She smiled again. 'Fine.'

A shadow loomed over them. Looking up, she saw it was Bart, a strange look on his face. 'Has Dr. Pipp rang through for me?' he asked curtly.

Dennis was walking away, the usual look of hostility on his face that he wore when Bart was around. He paused and looked over his shoulder. 'He was leaving at noon today . . .' he said and walked away.

Bart frowned. Looking at him, Creena's heart skipped a beat. Oh, how dear he was, how very dear. That strong calm face, that gentle mouth, that obstinate chin. That long fair hair—when had he last visited the hairdresser?—those blue eyes that seemed able to pierce any defence.

'No package come for me?' he asked and when Creena shook her head, he thrust his hand worriedly through his hair. 'Can't understand it. Pipp promised to send me down the findings of that bacteriological test that came down from Johannesburg. He had a new theory about Mrs. Carter . . . frankly, she's—'

'Dr. Darling . . .' The African doctor's voice was low but penetrating. She came swiftly down the corridor, immaculate in her white coat, her dark beautiful face perturbed. 'Please come at once . . . Mrs. Carter . . . haemorrhage . . .' Bart was off down the corridor like a shot—with that slow-looking swift movement.

The telephone bell shrilled . . . an African delivery boy arrived with two sheafs of flowers—Matron came bustling because someone had complained about the food and had said she was not on her proper diet—and then Dr. Hall walked in calmly, lifting his hand in greeting to his daughter who sat, face flushed, red-gold hair ruffled, trying to cope with three things at once.

'Bart 'phoned me . . .' he explained quietly to Creena. 'Car's in garage so got a lift up but don't wait for me. Get a lift back . . .' He disappeared down the corridor.

It was long past half-past four before Creena could put the cover on her typewriter, run a comb through her hair, carefully outline her mouth with lipstick and powder her nose, picking up her cardigan and handbag, turning to the door, just as Janice came bustling by, her white hair untidy, face flushed.

'Something wrong?' Creena asked sympathetically.

Janice paused in mid-flight. 'Just about everything. That poor Mrs. Carter . . . if only they had let Dr. Tyson operate as he suggested but Dr. Pipp said she'd never stand up to the shock. Janice's eyes glowed. 'Dennis . . . Dr. Tyson I mean, is such a miraculous surgeon— I'm sure he could have pulled her through. Oh, no . . .' she moaned as a bell shrilled urgently. 'That's for me . . . will the day never end?' She rushed off down the corridor.

Creena stopped in the town, going into the store to get a shampoo sachet and some new nail varnish, chatting with Mrs. Allsop—then seeing Mrs. Isipin and trying to avoid her but without success.

'Have you met this . . . this Laura—yet, Creena?' Mrs. Isipin asked, blocking the entrance to the store. 'No one seems to have seen her but—'

Creena's face flamed with quick anger. 'Of course they haven't,' she snapped rudely. She met Mrs. Isipin's outraged glare with an equal icy look. 'For the simple reason, Mrs. Isipin,' she said slowly and with deliberate coldness. 'She is not here. She happens to be in England with her husband.'

There was instant disbelief in the accusing eyes watching her. 'Who says so?'

'Dr. Darling told me so,' Creena said flatly. 'If anyone should know, he should.'

Mrs. Isipin pursed her mouth. 'Well, his mother says—'

Creena drew a deep breath. 'Mrs. Isipin . . .' Her voice was suddenly pleading. 'Have you found a single person in town who *has* seen Laura?' She watched Mrs. Isipin's face change. 'I see, that struck you also. I suddenly realized that I was always hearing about her second-hand. Someone said that they had heard she was quite something . . . someone else had heard something else. So I asked Bart . . . I mean, Dr. Darling, and he told me that

215

Laura's husband is a doctor and a great friend of his and he has gone, with his wife, to England, on a refresher course.' Creena paused, for breath.

'It's curious you should say that,' Mrs. Isipin said very slowly. 'Do you know, I had begun to wonder where she could be if she existed. This isn't such a large place and none of the hotels . . .' She paused while two flags of crimson showed in her cheeks as if ashamed of what she had unwittingly admitted. 'I can't understand it, though. His mother . .' She frowned thoughtfully. 'She hasn't seen Laura either, she told me. But who would want to invent such a story . . .'

Creena shrugged, seized her parcel and prepared for escape. 'Your guess is as good as mine,' she said with a nonchalance she was far from feeling. ' 'Bye . . .'

When she got home, she was dismayed to find Mrs. Darling installed in a chair on the shady stoep. She looked very small and miserable, hunched in her chair, wearing a grey shapeless frock, tugging at the rings on her fingers with unhappy hands.

'Is Bartie all right, dear?' were her first words.

Creena hesitated. She longed for a quick shower and a change of clothes. She could never get used to what she called 'the hospital smell,' and hated wearing a dress she had worn to work, 'Fine, Mrs. Darling,' she said cheerfully.

'Is that Mrs. Carter all right?' Mrs. Darling went on. 'I know Dr. Pipp was very worried at leaving her. I mean, Bartie is quite good but he is a young doctor . . .'

Something seemed to snap inside Creena. 'Mrs. Darling,' she said very earnestly. 'I think you forget that Bart is not a boy. He is a man of thirty-five, a fine doctor and surgeon. Quite the finest doctor we have in the hospital . . .'

Mrs. Darling was gaping at her, her mouth wide open, reminding Creena irresistibly of a fledgeling bird in a nest with his beak opened to its widest capacity. Creena cooled down a little and went on slowly:

'Dr. Pipp would not have put Mrs. Carter in Bart's hands had he not been completely confident of Bart's ability to cope with any emergency,' she spoke firmly but inside her, a small fear sparked. It was more than likely that Mrs. Carter would die—obviously that had been Dr. Pipp's fear—and if she did die, then would Mrs. Darling seize that as another weapon with which to wreck her son's medical career?

'You seem to have a high opinion of my son,' Mrs. Darling said, her voice suspicious.

'We all have . . . at the hospital,' Creena added lamely and was suddenly aware that her mother was standing in the doorway, hearing everything, her face puzzled. 'We all respect and admire Dr. Darling very much,' Creena

217

finished stiffly, passed her mother, dropping a light kiss on her cheek, and hurried to her room.

Was there nothing to be done? No way to keep Mrs. Darling from ruining Bart's life? Creena flung herself down on the bed and beat the pillow hard with frustrated impotent hands. Surely there must be some way some means of making Mrs. Darling see . . .

Dr. Hall was late for dinner. His arrival was a welcome relief to his family for Mrs. Darling had been talking throughout the meal in her whining affected voice, telling Norma never to marry a doctor, commiserating with Creena on her *plight*, telling Mike how thankful his mother must be that he was going to be a farmer, such a nice stable sort of life, so near to earth, both feet on the ground.

Creena saw Mike making a valiant effort to answer politely—the way Mrs. Darling spoke, no one but a soft-brained yokel would want to be a farmer; saw Norma sulking, Mrs. Hall being very polite and friendly. And then the doctor arrived, looking weary and sad. He made his apologies and Mrs. Darling was coy. 'We know you can't help it, Doctor . . . have you been advising my son?'

Creena's father drank his soup quickly. 'He has been advising me . . .' he said with a wry smile. 'No matter how hard you try, it is difficult to keep up with the latest drugs and techniques. Your son, ma'am, is a very fine doctor . . .' He spoke in an old-fashioned, rather pedantic way and Creena saw her mother's face grow worried and knew it was a sign that her father was very tired, very near the end of his tether.

'So Creena has been telling me,' Mrs. Darling said, her voice shrill with forced gaiety. 'It seems she thinks I don't appreciate him enough. I know he is a good doctor but he is a very bad son. Dr. Hall—couldn't you tell him that the only sensible thing to do is to leave here and go back to England? He is so talked about—all this scandal frightens me. He could be struck off the rolls and—'

'For what?' Dr. Hall asked quietly. 'For being a good doctor and doing his job properly?'

Mrs. Darling's face was bright red. 'Of course I don't mean that. I mean all this talk about Laura . . .' She said the word distastefully. 'Chasing him all over the country, threatening to wreck his career . . .'

'A man can't go on running away, Mrs. Darling,' Creena's father said quietly, giving his wife a quick smile as she quietly replaced his plate. 'Good—roast chicken, my favourite dish,' he went on, giving his three children a quick conspiratorial smile, knowing how tired they were of chicken. Have you thought that if this woman wants to chase him, she can follow him to England. Much the best thing for him to do is to call her bluff . . .'

'Call her bluff?' Mrs. Darling echoed, her voice startled.

'Yes. That's what I said,' Dr. Hall went on cheerfully. 'She hasn't a leg to stand on. All doctors know these predatory women and no one would condemn him . . .'

Mrs. Darling looked even more puzzled and Creena wondered if she knew what predatory meant. She for one, did not! She was burning to tell Mrs. Darling that they knew the truth—that she had invented the anonymous letter and Laura's arrival here, simply to wreck her son's career. Anger burned inside Creena and made her feel so ill that when her mother looked at her, she mumbled an excuse and rushed from the room.

She felt better later and joined the others in the large cool lounge. Dr. Hall was lying back in his chair, eyes closed while Creena's mother was valiantly carrying on a one-sided conversation with Mrs. Darling who appeared to be sulking. They were all startled when Bart walked in. His hair on end, his face drawn with deeply-etched lines of weariness and unhappiness.

His mother was on her feet. 'Bartie . . . you're very late. How is she?' she demanded quickly.

Bart stared at her and Creena was sure he saw nothing, no one.

'Please,' he said and lifted a hand wearily. 'I'd rather not . . . not talk about it. We couldn't save her, Doc . . .' he said, his voice almost a plea, as he looked at the older man.

Creena's father was on his feet. 'We never expected to,' he said. 'Pipp knew it was a chance in a million. Perhaps if that test result had got through.'

'She's dead,' Mrs. Darling said tragically.

Neither of the two men looked at her or gave any sign of hearing her.

'Come with me, son . . .' Dr. Hall said gently. 'We both need a drink. My wife kept your dinner hot . . .'

'I don't feel like food . . .' Bart began.

'Of course you don't but you still have to eat . . .' Dr. Hall said and, with his arm lightly round the younger man's shoulder, led him to the dining-room.

There was silence. Mrs. Darling mopped her eyes. 'I only wanted to help him . . .'

'I know,' Creena's mother said gently. 'But there is nothing one can do. They always take it as a personal failure. Mrs. Carter was always very delicate. For years, Dr. Pipp has fought to keep her going . . .'

'Dr. Tyson wanted to operate,' Mrs. Darling said unexpectedly. 'Bartie wouldn't let him. Maybe if he had . . .'

Creena saw her mother close her eyes for a second and guessed what she was thinking and then her mother was smiling. 'We shan't help by sitting here moping, Mrs. Darling, I promised my neighbour we'd go over for

221

bridge if that suits you?'

'Bridge?' Mrs. Darling brightened immediately. 'I'd love it. I get so bored all day long up in that cottage by the hospital. No where to go, no one to talk to and at night, Bartie is too tired to take me out . . .'

'There isn't anywhere to go,' Creena said quietly.

Mrs. Darling looked at her. 'You young people seem to find enough to do from all accounts,' she said tartly.

'I've got your wrap, Mrs. Darling,' Creena's mother was saying. 'Shall we go now?'

It was a relief to have the room to herself. To lie back in the chair and close her eyes, listening to the low rumble of distant voices and know that Bart was there—that she was bound to see him later. She was tired after the busy day and must have dozed for when she awoke, the two men were in the room talking quietly and she had a light wrap over her. She lay back in the chair, very still, keeping her eyes closed, wondering what Bart was like when he was with another man.

They were still talking about Mrs. Carter. Medical jargon she could not understand. Bart kept saying that he wished the test results had reached him, that he could not understand it, Dr. Pipp had promised to send them down.

'I doubt if they would have helped,' Creena heard her father say.

'You're probably right but we'll never know,

222

now . . .'

Creena opened her eyes and yawned and the two men began to tease her.

'The poor child works so hard,' her father laughed.

'You must be tired,' Creena said and regretted it. The last time she had said that to Bart he had snubbed her. Today he nodded and ran his hand through his hair.

'I am—at that. Thanks be I'm not on duty tonight. It's Tyson's turn . , .' he said wearily.

She jumped up. 'Like some coffee, Dad? Bart? I would . . .'

She went out to the kitchen, opened the fridge and took out the milk. It would take no time at all on the hot plate of the Esse. She lifted the heavy lid just as the telephone bell rang.

'I'll take it, Dad,' she called, eager to save her weary father the effort of getting out of his deep comfortable chair. It was Janice on the telephone from the hospital.

'Is Dennis there?' she asked, her voice urgent.

'No . . .' Crecna hesitated. 'isn't he on call?'

'Yes, he is but . . . I thought I heard him say he would call for you,' Janice said accusingly.

Creena remembered the little incident that Bart had interrupted. Dennis saying he would be busy that night and then loudly arranging to meet her. She knew swift momentary anger with Dennis for placing her in such a position

223

and equal anger with Janice for thinking she had the right to cross-examine her.

'He couldn't make it,' she said abruptly. 'I don't know where he is.'

'I've got to find him,' Janice sounded desperate. 'Your father is dead tired, I don't want to call on him and I can't trace Dr. Darling...'

Creena hesitated. It would be easy enough to replace the receiver. Bart was dead tired. If it was Dennis's night on duty, he had no right to go off...

But she was beaten before she began to fight, she knew that. A doctor's daughter was well-trained in what was right and wrong where patients were concerned. 'Dr. Darling is here but he's very tired...'

'Thanks be—put him on the line,' Janice snapped.

Reluctantly Creena held out the receiver to Bart who shrugged and smiled at her and took it. His face sobered, he gave some brief instructions, slammed down the receiver and turned to them.

'Bad fire out at the Mill. They're sending in patients but several men are trapped and I've got to go at once...' he said.

'But Tyson,' Creena's father said, heaving himself reluctantly to his feet.

'Can't be found. They thought he was with Creena...'

Creena's cheeks were hot. 'He—he called it

224

off.'

Both the men were staring at her strangely and then Bart turned away.

'Could you run Mother home for me, Creena . . . I may not be back until late.' He hesitated. 'I hate to ask you to do this, sir, but . . .' He turned to Creena's father.

'I know—I know. All in a night's work, son. I'll go straight up to the hospital and organize things. You'll have to give me a lift—car's in the garage . . .' He turned to Creena. 'Tell your mother, darling. I'll probably sleep up there . . .'

'If you're lucky,' Bart said and strode out of the house without even a farewell look or word for Creena who stood there, watching them go.

The house seemed horribly still. She pressed her hands to her face and in the darkness, before her eyes were a million sparkling fireworks. A fire . . . men trapped. She began to shiver. Bart would be in danger—terrible danger . . .

The falling limb of a tree, burning still as it fell . . . the sudden onslaught of the fire as the wind suddenly changed and men were trapped . . .

She drew a long shuddering breath. This is what it meant to love a man. This shuddering helpless fear—this knowledge that you had to sit back and wait. And then she knew what she must do.

She hurried to the kitchen, opening a

cupboard, pulling out tall urns, putting on kettles of water. They had about ten thermos flasks, that would do for a start and if she took out urns filled with boiling water, she could reheat them out there.

Men fighting fires always needed tea . . . That was something she could do. Mrs. Darling would just have to stay there the night, the spare room was always ready. Hastily she scrawled a note for her mother and propped it up against the clock, hurriedly changed into jeans and a thin shirt and went out to her car. Thanks be, she had had it filled with petrol that morning.

She felt much happier once she was driving. She was on her way to be with Bart. That, she knew now, was all that mattered.

CHAPTER SIXTEEN

Creena had seen many fires—but always from a distance. This was very different. Clouds of billowing smoke—the horrible crackling sound as the fire swept through the growing trees—the sudden crack as a branch fell—the groups of natives beating out the fire with wet sacks—the Mill's fire-fighting squad with their hoses and chemical extinguishers. Crowds of people all milling around in seeming disorder but Creena soon recognized the practised discipline that controlled them.

The manager saw her and told her where she could set up her tea canteen. His good-looking face was smeared with smoke, his khaki jacket and shorts grimy, he looked intolerably weary. 'It's good of you to come,' he said in a rather curt manner, 'but you must keep out of the danger zone. You could be a liability rather than an asset . . . I'll send word round that you're there . . .'

Creena confessed to herself that she was not sorry when told to retreat to a safe distance but as she stood there, boiling water on the primus stove to replenish the urns, handing out cups, washing them up quickly in the bowl she had brought with her, she kept looking into the inferno of flames she was gazing down on and wondering where Bart was. When she had a moment to spare, she would ask each smoke-smeared man who came up if he had seen the doctor but no one had. It was as if an iron-hand clutched her heart, slowly, agonizingly squeezing it. Had Bart already been hurt and no one found him? The smell of the smoke and burned wood choked her—the curling red-tinged plumes of smoke drifting over the tree tops seemed like evil fingers reaching out to destroy.

'Bart,' she cried joyously when at last she saw him. He was helping a man along, taking his weight. Creena heard his voice first and he said a good cup of tea would help . . . and then he saw Creena.

'What the . . . what are you doing here?' he demanded harshly.

It was like a slap in the face. Somehow her romantic dream was slaughtered by the way he glared at her, the anger in his voice. She had been so glad to see him—to have her fears laid to rest—to know that he was all right.

The accountant who was gulping down the tea thirstily looked at her.

'That was just what I needed. You really are an angel.' He smiled at her. Creena knew him slightly and she was shocked at his appearance. He leaned against the car, wiping the black soot from his face. Then he turned to Bart.

'Thanks, old man. If you hadn't found me . . .' He looked at Creena. 'I got a crack on the head from a falling branch and no one saw me. Luckily this chap did. Nothing broken—I just feel muzzy.'

Bart was hesitating. 'Look—there could be some internal damage, you'd better go slow and report to the hospital . . .'

'I will—I will, don't fuss,' the accountant said snappily. 'This isn't the time. Creena, here, will look after me.'

'Bart—Bart.' Creena's mouth was dry as she took the empty cup from the tall angry man. 'You . . .' She looked up at him worriedly, aware that Philip Seers, the accountant, had slumped into her car, was resting his head in his hands, paying them no attention. Suddenly

228

the frightened words fell out of Creena's mouth. 'Bart—please . . . please be careful . . .'

His hands were suddenly hard on her shoulders, his fingers digging into the flesh. 'You're a fine one to talk,' he said harshly. 'Deliberately running into danger like this . . .'

Her mouth was dry but she found the courage she needed as she stared at him. 'I had to be near you . . . I couldn't bear it if . . . if anything happened to you. Bart—Bart . . .' Her voice rose. 'Please . . . please take care . . .'

His hands fell away from her shoulders. 'Don't talk like that,' he said harshly. 'You're like all women. You sound just like my mother . . .'

She stood very still, watching him as he plunged back into the mêlée. Her hands pressed against her mouth, as she fought back the tears. She had shown him for the second time how much she loved him—and he had tossed that love right back into her face.

Dimly she heard the sound of other cars arriving—soon she was just part of a group of women who had brought out food and drinks for the men who were fighting the fire. Mrs. Isipin was there, her waspiness forgotten as she began to organize things. Her acid voice was hard but there was no unkindness there as she talked to the Manager and began to arrange a shuttle service to get the less-badly injured victims back to the hospital. Already the two ambulances were working full-time—

hurrying back along the narrow road that crept round the side of the mountains, through the trees, crossing the small rivers. Creena drove Philip and two other men back to the hospital and then went back to the fire—but by now it was beginning to come under control and some of the frightening urgency had lifted. It was some hours before she got home and could tumble exhausted into bed, shutting Bart out of her mind, telling herself that she must accept the fact that there was no room for a woman in his life.

At the hospital next day, everything was chaotic. Patients lying on mattresses in the corridor, on the stoep—the nurses run off their feet. Creena lent a hand as much as she could, acting as ward-maid, doing all the jobs that the nurses had no time to do. She met Dennis coming out of one of the private wards, an immaculately-dressed Dennis who looked at her unblinkingly.

'Dennis—where were you last night?' she said without thinking. 'We needed you so much . . .' She still felt sick when she thought of how her father had looked that morning when someone drove him home and he stumbled up to the house and into bed. Her father and the African woman had been the only two doctors at the hospital and apparently the night had been one long nightmare of burns to be treated, limbs amputated, transfusions given.

Dennis glowered. 'Not you as well, Creena! 'I'm sick and tired of the question.'

Anger flared up within her. 'You were on duty—you should have left your address,' she told him.

He frowned. 'For crying out loud . . . since when have you had the right to lecture me? How could I know there was going to be a fire? Darling is always around so why should I spoil my fun . . .'

'Your . . . your fun . . .' Creena choked over the words. She pulled off her engagement ring and gave it to him. 'I can't go on with this farce even to help you, Dennis.'

He smiled thinly and pocketed the ring. 'Okedoke. In any case, there's no point. I've blotted my copy-book for good and all with the old buzzard. She's mad as hell with me . . .'

'Can you blame her?' Creena asked and stalked off down the corridor.

Her finger felt curiously light and she had a sense of freedom. Now Bart would see . . .

She stood still, eyes stinging, as she fought for control. How much longer could she go on fooling herself? Hadn't she practically thrown herself in Bart's arms? And he had made it plain enough that he was not interested.

There was trouble on every side that day. Mrs. Carter's relations had descended on the hospital like an avalanche of furies, demanding an inquiry, accusing the hospital of negligence. Mrs. Crampton had risen from her sick bed and looked like a walking skeleton, her eyes deeply sunken, her hands trembling as she leant on two sticks.

'We have never had such a thing happen in my hospital,' she kept saying.

Meg came into Creena's office, so angry she could hardly speak. 'They are accusing Bart of letting Mrs. Carter die—saying that had Dennis operated—'

'Dr. Pipp was against an operation,' Creena pointed out, 'and she was his patient. If only that pathology test result had come through in time . . .'

'What test?' Mrs. Crampton demanded harshly. They had not heard her approach and she was leaning on the small counter that separated the office from the hall.

Creena explained. 'Dr. Pipp said he would send it down if it arrived before he left—I imagine he would tell Mrs. Pipp to do so . . .'

Mrs. Crampton's mouth tightened. 'Put me through to Rosalie . . .'

It was quite a job to get Rosalie Pipp—her housegirl who spoke little English seemed afraid to get her, kept saying the Missus was asleep and would be very cross. 'So will I be,' Mrs. Crampton snapped into the telephone. She gave it back to Creena. 'Go on trying, girl. I'll be in my little room.' She hobbled off down the corridor, her back erect as if a poker had been swallowed.

'She's pretty mad,' Meg said complacently.

Startled, Creena looked at her, hugging the telephone in one hand.

'You sound pleased.'

'I am,' Meg said. 'This will finish Dennis Tyson.'

'What do you mean . . .?' Creena saw that Meg was looking pointedly at the bare ringless finger on her left hand.

'I thought you knew and that was why you'd broken the engagement,' Meg said.

'Knew what?' Creena snapped.

'Well—that Dennis and Rosalie Pipp were at that new hotel in the Blue Mountains—the Askari, I think it is called. Then went to dinner and got home about four o'clock this morning.'

'I—didn't know . . .' Creena said slowly.

'I'm sorry if it has upset you,' Meg said quickly.

Creena smiled. 'I'm not upset. I didn't love Dennis . . .'

'Then why—'

'I'll tell you some time. I'd better try and get Rosalie Pipp now . . .' Creena said. Relentlessly she talked to the frightened housegirl and finally made her call Rosalie. Rosalie sounded irritable and sleepy but startled when she heard Mrs. Crampton wanted her. Couldn't it wait, she demanded, but Creena said that Mrs. Crampton had insisted that she speak to her. So Rosalie agreed and Creena put her through to Mrs. Crampton's little office, smiling a little as she did. Although Dr. Pipp had quite a number of private patients, he also needed Mrs. Crampton's good-will and so he had taught Rosalie always to be on good terms with the old lady.

Creena was startled about twenty minutes later to get a message from Mrs. Crampton, asking her to contact Dr. Tyson and tell him to go to her office *at once.* Not wishing to speak to him personally, Creena sent an orderly with the message and five minutes later, saw Dennis walking down the corridor to Mrs. Crampton's room.

A long distance 'phone call came through—then some visitors arrived to see one of the badly burned patients—nurses were constantly hurrying by the little office—the whole hospital seemed tense.

Creena was amazed when the orderly came and found her in one of the wards. His black face looked tired and almost grey for the African staff had worked full out all night and many of them had not slept at all. Mrs. Crampton wanted to see her.

Unperturbed, Creena went to the little office and had a shock when she saw Dennis still there, his face sulky, his eyes smouldering.

'Shut the door, Creena, and sit down.' Mrs. Crampton's voice was like the rasping of a saw that needed oiling. She looked more like a witch than ever, behind her desk that almost filled the room. 'Sit down . . . As you are engaged to Dennis, I think it only fair to tell you,' she went on remorselessly, ignoring Creena's attempted denial, 'that I have asked him to hand in his resignation.'

Creena caught her breath, looking at Dennis quickly. This would ruin his plans.

'I am also,' the old lady went on, her voice suddenly uncertain, 'no longer going to make him a beneficiary in my will. As you doubtless know, I was going to leave my hospital in his hands. I am not—now.' Her voice grated.

'But Mrs. Crampton . . .' Creena began. 'Why—'

'Because I do not consider him a fit person to have charge of my hospital,' Mrs. Crampton said flatly. 'Last night he should have been on call—instead he goes off with a married woman and neglects to leave information as to where he is . . .' Her eyes flicked over Creena's face. 'I see you already know that. Do you know, also, that he could have been the cause of Mrs. Carter's death?' Her voice rose. 'Dr. Pipp asked his wife to send down a letter from the Pathology Laboratory—and she says she gave it to Dennis . . .'

'That is a lie,' Dennis drawled, but Creena knew, with a sense of shock, that it might not be. Who could trust his word?

'One of you is a liar,' Mrs. Crampton said.

Dennis moved impatiently. 'Those path. findings were not important. I knew the only solution was to operate—'

235

'Wanted your way—regardless of whether it was right or wrong,' Mrs. Crampton said in a cutting voice. She turned to Creena. 'As his future wife, I feel you should know these things.'

'She isn't my future wife,' Dennis said almost contemptuously. He smiled and Creena shivered. 'It was an engagement of convenience. Creena didn't want Dr. Darling to know that she was in love with him . . .' He ignored Creena's low startled cry of distress and went on: 'And I wanted you to think that I was going to settle down and marry a nice girl like Creena. I'd rather be dead,' he said with a vicious anger that made Creena feel sick. She crouched in her chair, hand to her mouth, as Dennis revealed himself. Dennis was smiling again, that cruel ruthless smile. 'You see, Mrs. Crampton, right from the beginning, I planned to make you dependent on me, to make you leave me the hospital. I don't need it now. I've been in negotiation with a syndicate of Johannesburg business men who plan to build a nursing home in the neighbourhood and I'll be in complete charge there with no old women telling me what to do . . .' He almost spat the words out.

Mrs. Crampton had gone very pale. 'You planned——'

'It all,' he put his hands on his hips and straddled a chair, looking pleased with himself. 'It was all very well worked out—the first snag was when I hurt my arm—then the next was when Darling ingratiated himself with you. However I coped with that very well. I—'

'You wrote that anonymous letter to Mrs. Darling,' Creena gasped.

He nodded. 'Yes—and I brought Laura here . . .' he began to laugh.

'She isn't here,' Creena said. 'She is in England.'

He went on laughing. 'I know—but you all believed she was here, didn't you? Credulous lot of fools . . .' he said contemptuously.

'You were very clever,' Creena said.

He looked pleased. 'I am—very clever. I am a brilliant surgeon, a good physician and a very clever man . . .'

'You are a fool, Dennis Tyson,' Mrs. Crampton said harshly. 'You can't go through life thrusting people on one side, having everything your way. One day you'll pay for it. You'll be like me—a lonely . . .'

He looked at her coldly. 'I'll never be like you. How I stood you all these years, I don't know . . .'

Creena was on her feet as she saw Mrs. Crampton turn pale, her hand fly to her heart. 'Dennis . . .' she cried in alarm.

He was at the door, looking at them. 'Don't worry,' he said quietly. 'There's nothing wrong with her heart. She's just a hypochondriac—a neurotic, love-starved old fool.' He shut the door with a slam.

The two women stared at one another. Mrs. Crampton's hand fell away from her heart. Her face changed, she seemed to relax. 'I'm sorry, Creena,' she said slowly.

Creena smiled. 'It's all right. As he said, I didn't love him. He said he had great plans for the hospital, enlargements, he seemed so sincere. I'm . . .' Her face was suddenly red. 'I owe you an apology for letting you believe I was engaged to him. It was cheating . . .'

Mrs. Crampton moved her hand vaguely. 'He could be so charming,' she said sadly.

Going back to her office, Creena thought that described Dennis perfectly. *He could be so charming.* What would her mother say when she learned the truth about her wonderful Dennis.

The days passed slowly. Dennis left the hospital and the small town seethed with rumours, most of them very remote from the truth. Bart was very busy at the hospital and never came to visit the Halls. His mother had moved down to one of the hotels, telling everyone plaintively that she had been so lonely and of course, a doctor's mother was the last one to ever see her son. Somehow, Creena managed to avoid seeing Bart during the day. Or was it, she wondered, if he was avoiding her? He worked long hard hours and Meg dropped in whenever she had a spare second, to tell Creena how wonderful Bart was.

Somehow Creena got through the days. She had secretly made plans and was finding out what it would cost to take a small flatlet in Durban and get a job there. She knew that if Bart was to stay on at the hospital—and it seemed very likely—then she could not stay in Klomati—could not bear to live near him, to see him all the time, to know that he had rejected her love.

Unfortunately love was a strange thing. Even being rejected, did not stop you from loving someone with your whole heart. She still trembled a little when she heard his voice—could still feel that sweet breathlessness when he entered a room. She still longed to tell him to get his hair cut—she still wanted to trace that stubborn line of his jaw with her finger—still wanted to look after him . . . Surely pride should wipe away these feelings? Surely—pride . . . But it didn't. She still ached with the pain of being rejected, still had that desolate, life-is-not-worth-living-without-him feeling. Would it ever go? How could she bear it . . .

A new doctor arrived at the hospital to take Dennis's place. A young, chubby-faced friendly man with the strange name of Elder Catt. He spread an aura of cheerfulness throughout the hospital and was immediately on Christian name terms with everyone. A few days later, Meg came to Creena. 'This will surprise you,' she said, her serene face excited. 'I'm going to

England.'

'You are?' Creena cried, feeling a pang of envy. New lands—new people. 'But—'

'What about my mother?' Meg said cheerfully. 'Everything is working out well. Bart, the honey that he is, has found an old ladies' home for her. It isn't free, you know,' she said a little stiffly, 'but we can manage. Mother says she will enjoy the company of people of her own age. I . . . I hadn't realized until Bart pointed it out that Mother is very much alone out in our little place. I love the quietness here when I'm off duty but she has it all the time. I'm going to take some new courses, in England. Isn't it thrilling?' she asked.

Creena agreed that it was and watched Meg almost dance down the corridor with happiness. The power of a good man, she thought. Bart immediately recognized the trouble in that home and has put it right.

There were changes everywhere. Janice, going round looking like a ghost, had handed in her resignation. She was going back to Johannesburg.

'More men, there,' she told Creena with a wry smile. 'I shan't only have one personable man about whom to make a fool of myself.'

'You aren't the only one,' Creena said.

Janice smiled in sympathy. 'I know. Dennis had a way . . .'

Creena nodded, grateful that no one—

except Dennis—seemed to have guessed her secret.

One very wet day—for suddenly, as was their way, the rains had come—Creena, sheltering underneath the same umbrella as her father as they walked round the garden, confided in him the whole story. He listened patiently.

'I can't understand a sensible girl like you falling for that story of Dennis's,' he said bluntly, looking down at her. 'That line about Bart and his wealthy mother. She is absolutely dependent on Bart and her debts nearly drive him mad. As for Dennis being an orphan— that's a lot of lies. He's got two very nice parents. They live in East London and he visits them about once a year.'

'But . . . but why does he lie about it?' Creena asked. Her feet slushed through the mud, great streams of water raced down their mountain-side garden but the air was fresh and cool after the intense heat of the past weeks.

Her father shrugged. 'Ashamed of them, I guess. He was a social climber, you know. They have a small store—not a big one, that you can be proud of,' he said bitterly. 'I've met them—nice homely folk and so very proud of him.'

'Daddy—I must go away—right away,' Creena said abruptly.

Her father was closing the umbrella,

shaking it rather ineffectively before putting it in a corner of the stoep. Samson shook himself far more effectively near them, evoking cries of protest from both father and daughter, and Rudi came in, shivering and looking so pathetic, that Creena picked up an old towel she always kept in the window seat they now used for storage on the wide stoep and rubbed him dry. Just as they had shed their macintoshes, Quido arrived; the black labrador had a long silk coat and he shook himself delicately, like a ballet dancer, but still succeeded in making everyone very wet.

'Dogs,' Dr. Hall said in mute dismay.

Creena smiled at him. 'They're your weakness, darling. You know you'd hate life without them. Seriously, Dad—I think I ought to get a job right away from . . .'

He looked worried. 'Don't rush into things, Creena. Look,' his face brightened as if he had just had a good idea, 'why don't we all go up to Lourenço Marques for a weekend? Wouldn't that make a nice break?'

She was tempted to say that it was just a postponement and not a settlement of her problem but, as she looked at his tired face, she loved him so much that it hurt. He was only trying to help her.

'That would be lovely, Daddy,' she said excitedly. 'We haven't been there for ages. We could all go?'

'I don't see why not,' her father said. 'Let's

go in and see what everyone says . . .'

Everyone was enthusiastic and they planned to go the following weekend if the rains let up. They did and it was on a perfect cloudless day that the big shabby car, filled with the Halls, set off early in the morning. As they started to climb the steep mountain roads that led to the border and entry into Mozambique, Creena felt a lifting of her tension. At least for three days she would not have to brace herself in case Bart walked into the room—would not have to watch her face lest it betray her—not have this tense eager longing to see him all mixed up with the fear lest he see through her thin defence.

It was a pleasant weekend—they danced at the nightclubs, they bathed on the white sandy beaches, walking out miles in the tepid waters, shouting and laughing a lot, sitting under striped umbrellas on the pavements of the town, watching people walk by. It was so totally different from their usual life in Klomati that they all enjoyed it. Even Norma seemed to cheer up and to begin to enjoy life again; she had been in the doldrums ever since Dennis's departure and somehow, irrationally, she had always implied that it was all Creena's fault that Dennis had left the hospital.

They got home in the early evening and the first thing Creena saw was the message by the telephone. Would she ring a certain number immediately. Her foolish heart lifted—and then sank when she recognized the number. Why did Mrs. Crampton want her to telephone?

Violet, the housegirl, smart in a crisp starched apron, her tiny white cap perched at a jaunty angle on her black tight little curls, told her that this Missus had called six times that day and seemed very cross.

Shrugging a little, Creena called the old lady. Mrs. Crampton's voice was urgent. 'I must see you immediately, Creena . . .'

'Won't tomorrow . . .' Creena was tired after the ninety mile journey—dusty, longing for a shower.

'No—it will be too late. Please come at once,' Mrs. Crampton said and Creena heard the click as she must have replaced the receiver.

Driving along the mountain roads, Creena wondered what could be the reason for this urgency. What did she mean—*it will be too late?*

In the big luxurious house, Mrs. Crampton looked older than ever.

'Creena—you must help me,' she said desperately. 'Is it true what Dennis said? That you love Bart Darling?'

It was as if Creena's face was on fire. Her cheeks burned painfully. She looked into the black beady eyes of the old woman and knew that she had to tell the truth. 'Yes, I do . . .' she said softly.

Mrs. Crampton's claw-like hands clutched her arm. 'You must help me to stop him, then ...'

'Stop him?'

'Yes—he's packing tonight to leave us,' Mrs. Crampton said. 'He's found us another doctor and he is taking his mother back to England.'

'Bart is going . . . to England . . .' Creena said very slowly. It was as if something had clicked in her brain and everything fell neatly in place.

Meg's excitement—excitement that she had thought even then was rather much for the occasion. Meg going to England—Bart, at last, taking his mother to England. It could only mean one thing. There was room for a woman in Bart's life—and that woman was Meg.

CHAPTER SEVENTEEN

Half an hour later, Creena and Mrs. Crampton were outside Bart's cottage. Creena had gone reluctantly, constantly saying that she had no influence over Bart, that she could do nothing. Mrs. Crampton had insisted—and then had pleaded.

'We need him so much, Creena. He is a good man as well as being a fine doctor. A hospital needs a man like that at its head. A man of ethics—a man we can respect . . .'

245

In the end, Creena had consented. Mrs. Crampton had gone first in her big luxurious car, driven by her chauffeur, while Creena had followed meekly behind.

Now as they stood on the tiny stoep, Creena felt like running away. She could not ask Bart to stay—not now she knew the truth, that he was in love with Meg.

Mrs. Crampton knocked and then opened the door in her usual imperious manner. The lounge, a small bleak-looking room with white-washed walls and dingy curtains was empty. Mrs. Crampton walked through it to the bedroom. The tall broad-shouldered man who was carefully folding a shirt and putting it in a suitcase, straightened and stared at them. If he felt surprise, he hid it well. His eyes flickered over Creena as if she had not been there.

'Dr. Darling . . .' Mrs. Crampton's voice was desperate. 'We've come to beg you to change your mind, to stay. We need you, Dr. Darling . . . need you so badly.' She gave him no time to speak but hurried on. 'I know that you and I have not always seen eye to eye. I admit that in many ways I am parsimonious—I have a plan—if you agree, I think it may solve our respective problems. I want this hospital to be a good one, to be renowned in memory of my dear late husband . . . but I have to be careful with my money. I plan to make it into a limited company and . . . and I want you to be the Managing Director . . .' She paused as if she

246

was offering him the Crown Jewels and expected him to be overwhelmed. But Bart's face did not lose its sternness. He waited for her to continue. 'You will be in complete charge—you . . .' Her voice faltered. 'Won't you stay, Dr. Darling? We respect you and . . .'

He spoke then. 'I did not notice much respect, Mrs. Crampton, when you had me up on the carpet about Mrs. Carter's death.'

Mrs. Crampton's pale cheeks were flushed. 'I was hasty. I always am hasty, I am afraid. Those people—they frightened me.'

'Nor do I feel that the town people respect me. I have recently heard full details of the gossip about me that swept the place,' his voice was cold with anger. 'I may be useful to you but . . . that is all.'

'It isn't all, Bart,' Creena said suddenly, the words exploding as it were. 'What of that little African girl who will one day be able to see with both eyes? You were the only one who thought of sending her to Baragwanath—what of little Elias . . . you know his legs are better already—what of . . . oh I can think of lots of things. Dad said you were the only sort of doctor that would be any good here—that you were dedicated and that was the important thing . . .'

He turned away, his face still cold. 'I am taking my mother back to England.'

'Are you sure she wants to go back, now?' Creena asked on the spur of the moment.

Something her mother had said about how much happier Mrs. Darling was at the hotel, gave her the idea.

'Quite sure,' Bart said. He half-smiled and indicated the telephone. 'Give her a ring if you need convincing.'

More to gain time than anything else, Creena obeyed. At last she was speaking to Mrs. Darling. 'I hear you are leaving tomorrow and going back to England,' Creena said abruptly. 'Are you glad?'

'Oh, Creena, I don't know what to do,' Mrs. Darling's voice in her ear was like a childish wail. 'I daren't tell Bartie. I've been begging him to take me home for months and months and now . . . I just don't know how to tell him I don't want to go. I've been thinking about the cold and the fogs and I've made some very nice friends here and . . . and there is even some talk of me going into partnership with a woman here—we plan to open a hat-shop. But how can I tell Bartie?' she wailed.

'Hold on,' Creena said. 'Here he is . . .' With a small triumphant smile, she gave the receiver to Bart. 'Your mother . . .'

She stood back, clasping her hands tightly as she watched his face change as he listened to his mother's fumbling words. 'Of course, it is all right, Mother,' he said gently. 'I am only too glad that you are so happy.' He replaced the receiver and with his back still turned to the two waiting women, he said: 'It makes no

248

difference. I shall go alone . . .'

The words fell into the room heavily. Mrs. Crampton turned away.

'I'm sorry,' she said and as they still stood there silently, Creena and Bart heard her car drive away.

Bart turned and stared at Creena. She did not know what she looked like but she felt rumpled and dusty and very very tired. Maybe it was the tiredness that inspired the childish accusation. 'So you lied all along, Bart—there is room for a woman in your life—and that woman is Meg.'

'Meg?' He stared at her, narrowing his eyes. 'Are you mad?'

'I have been. I believed you. Now you are going to England—with Meg. Are you ashamed to admit you love her? Why can't you both stay here . . .'

He crossed the room and his hands were on her shoulders. His fingers digging into her flesh. 'Are you mad?' he asked harshly. 'As for being ashamed . . . and for lying . . . why not admit the truth—that you and Dennis are going to be married the instant he gets another job. He wrote me from Cape Town, telling me so.'

She felt the colour drain from her face. 'Dennis wrote . . .' So Dennis with his sadistical cruelty, had planned to hurt them both even though it would make no difference to him.

'It's a lie,' she said indignantly. 'I was never in love with Dennis.'

His fingers dug into her flesh, his face was angry, eyes cold.

'Why go on lying. You were engaged to him . . .'

'Only for three months—I promised him I would be . . . it was to make Mrs. Crampton approve of him, to give him a chance to prove that he was steady and reliable . . . Oh, I've always . . . always loved you, Bartholomew Darling,' she said, angry now, twisting quickly and freeing herself from his fingers. 'And you've known it—and rejected me and I hate you . . . hate you . . .' She was half-crying with mixed anger and weariness and she turned blindly away and ran from the cottage.

She had not gone far before he caught her. He held her tightly—above them the dark sky was studded with brilliants, the new moon was a thin amber crescent. In the distance the drums were beginning to sound—somewhere close a dog howled—a cat cried—a bird stirred. It was a beautiful African night.

'When did I reject you?' he was asking, his arms holding her close.

She could not see his features—just a white blur above her. 'When . . . when I kissed you . . .' she said, her voice faltering. 'Then . . . then at the fire.'

'When you kissed me, I thought you were engaged to Dennis Tyson—at the fire, I was frightened . . . frightened for your safety. Don't you know that frightened love makes you very angry?'

'Love . . . love . . .' she repeated very slowly. 'Bart—are you telling me that you . . .'

'I am . . .' he said. The white blur that was his face came closer until she could see it no more, but only feel the warm hardness of his mouth against hers.

His arms held her very close and suddenly, her arms were round his neck. Even as she returned his kiss, her fingers wandered—now, she could stroke his hair, run her finger tenderly along the tiny curls. Tomorrow she would take him to have his hair cut—tomorrow, she would look at his socks, see if his buttons needed sewing on . . . at last, at long last, she was free to love him, to cherish him.

'Oh, Bart—Bart, darling . . .' she whispered. 'I can't believe it . . .'

'Neither can I . . .' he said and his arms tightened round her as his mouth hungrily found hers. 'We've wasted so much time . . .' he said.

'We've got so much time ahead of us . . .' she said joyously. 'Oh, Bart, isn't it wonderful . . . our whole lives before us. Oh, aren't we lucky . . .'

'I'm the lucky one . . .' he said and kissed her again.

A long while later, he released her and they

stood there, holding hands, staring at one another as if it was for the first time.

'Know something, Creena?' Bart said with a little nervous laugh, rather as if he found himself in a strange situation, a new one, 'I'll never be able to call you *Creena darling* in public or people will think I am a very odd sort of husband, calling my wife by her full name.'

'Creena Darling,' she echoed. 'What a perfectly wonderful name. Oh, Bart.' She clutched his arms, suddenly fearful of what might have been. 'We could have been parted—never met again. Oh, Bart . . . how could you? Would you really have gone away without telling me that you loved me?'

'I had no right—for Dennis wrote and told me . . .'

'Dennis!' Creena said with light scorn and tossed the name aside. 'We ought both to have known better than believe any of his lies. Couldn't you see . . .' She went closer and looked up into his face. 'Dennis knew I loved you—that's why he wrote to you like that. He wanted to hurt us . . . to think how nearly he succeeded . . .' she said slowly and shivered. 'I—' she laughed suddenly. 'Let's forget it and Dennis. I must ring Mrs. Crampton. She'll be so pleased . . . and then we must go and tell Daddy, he'll be thrilled . . .'

'But your mother?' Bart said ruefully. 'I think she always wanted you to marry Dennis.'

'Only because she is a sentimental

252

romantic,' Creena said gaily. 'Dennis could certainly lay on the charm and Mummy fell for it. Once she gets to know you, she won't be able to help loving you. No one could . . .' she said very softly.

She was in his arms again. 'Darling . . . darling . . .' he said. 'I only hope you'll always feel like that.' He sounded unsure, a little afraid. 'You know, darling, Mother could be right. It is a tough life being a doctor's wife . . .'

Creena held his head with her hands and lightly kissed each corner of his mouth. 'Don't be an idiot, Bart. Your mother doesn't know what she is talking about. Whatever career her husband had followed would have been wrong for her, poor soul. She doesn't seem to know that to hold a husband, you have to let him go.'

'You seem to know an awful lot . . .' he teased.

'I do,' she said triumphantly, 'but I've got an awful lot more to learn. One thing I do know, Bart, is that I wouldn't want to be anything but a doctor's wife—the wife of Dr. Darling.'

Chivers Large Print Direct

If you have enjoyed this Large Print book and would like to build up your own collection of Large Print books and have them delivered direct to your door, please contact **Chivers Large Print Direct**.

Chivers Large Print Direct offers you a full service:

✧ **Created to support your local library**

✧ **Delivery direct to your door**

✧ **Easy-to-read type and attractively bound**

✧ **The very best authors**

✧ **Special low prices**

For further details either call Customer Services on 01225 443400 or write to us at

Chivers Large Print Direct
FREEPOST (BA 1686/1)
Bath
BA1 3QZ